CW01468536

Contents

Reclusive Mountain Man's Mail Order Bride

Jacqueline Carmine

Elizabeth

Mornings are always busy at *Lenny's*. I've spent the last three years moving from place to place while living in my van. This isn't the first diner I've worked at, far from it. Finding odd jobs is easier in retail and food service, they are always shorthanded and if you've worked at one diner you've worked at them all.

I've lived in dozens of places since I bought my van a little over three years ago. No two places were exactly alike but after a year or so they all started to blur together. Without any roots I drifted aimlessly as my dream of travel morphed into a desire to find the one place I wanted to call home. Something about Crescent Ridge makes it different from the other cities and towns I've visited. Maybe it's the mountain air or it's the bubble of hometown pride everyone shares.

Two weeks as a waitress and already I know all the locals. Some better than others. Mama Mary was the first to welcome me and in fact she told Paul to give me a job here waiting tables. An angel with white hair who everyone fears. Her son routinely brings his family in for lunch. Daniel and Lily are adorable together with their children and their love story is straight out of a romance novel.

It's everything I wanted for myself.

Like Lily I signed up for Pearl's Mail Order Brides and I drove my van all the way out to Crescent Ridge to meet my match. I arrived a day early, knocked on his apartment door and was shocked to find a woman answer. Brett hadn't mentioned a sister or a cousin. He was only on the ridge to finish up a construction project for a travelling construction company. He said he had no family.

"You weren't supposed to be here till tomorrow," the woman said as she lounged in the doorway.

The oversized shirt she wore was from the same trade school that Brett had attended. I tried to rationalize it. Red flags were popping up and alarm bells were ringing but I was optimistic.

"I got here early," I told her. "Are you Brett's sister?"

"Babe!" A familiar voice called out from inside the apartment and after glancing over her shoulder the woman stepped into the hallway and closed the door behind her.

"I'm not his sister," she said with her mahogany brown eyes looking at me with pity. "We met at the bar last night in Bramble."

Glancing down at her bare legs I closed my eyes and counted to ten. Brett and I weren't a love match by any means. But I thought we had connected. He weaved a lovely tale of how we would travel the country together and eventually settle down and start a family. He complimented my brunette hair and called me pretty every chance we talked. He sent good morning texts and messaged me every day.

But a man serious about a woman doesn't go to bars looking for hookups.

"Thanks for your honesty," I told the woman.

I left that apartment building without a second glance. A day later and I never would have known. I would have married that smooth talking dirtbag. Fate was on my side.

Brett and I have bumped into one another since that day but either he doesn't recognize me or he's avoiding a confrontation. His disregard should hurt. I came all this way to marry the man. But only my pride is dented. And every day spent in Crescent Ridge works as a balm to soothe my bruised ego.

Now I work as a waitress, and I know everybody's dirty laundry. Like how Emma and Andrew met on a dating app looking for kinky sex and fell in love. Or how William accused his own mail order bride of trying to catfish him. Everyone in Crescent Ridge has a story.

Even me, the jilted mail order bride.

There's plenty of single men in Crescent Ridge but none have caught my eye. They're all built like they are carved from the mountains we live on. Chiseled and dripping with masculinity, there isn't a day that goes by that one of them doesn't try to get my number. They look at me like I'm a well-seasoned steak.

None of them leer or harass me. I don't think my boss would let them come back if they did. Paul is a grumpy one for sure. He might not have a high opinion of me, but he has an even lower one for any man who wanders inside intending to sample the waitstaff rather than the food.

I finish my shift later in the afternoon but unlike most days I don't go straight to the apartment I'm renting. I drive my van over to a trail Lily recommended this morning. It's the same one her sister met her own mountain man when he saved her during a storm. But unlike Gloria, I'm well prepared and the forecast is clear.

Best view in the entire mountain range. I'll see about that.

Jeb

It's a chilly day on the mountain. The leaves underfoot are crunchy, but I'm not worried about stealth today. I'm checking traps before working in the garden. No need to hunt a deer when the traps are catching plenty of rabbits.

The constant chatter of the mountain bluebirds follows me as I walk through the woods. It's as I'm checking the traps on the east side of my property that I hear an unusual sound. High pitched and off key, it takes a second for me to realize someone is singing.

And they cannot carry a tune to save their life.

I come into view of the main trail, and I spot the hiker making all the noise. Long brunette hair that shines in the sun catches my eye first before I take in her neon orange tank top and her khaki shorts. She's even wearing hiking boots. A seasoned hiker I decide, considering her clothing and the small knapsack on her back.

Never seen her before. A beautiful woman like her isn't easy to forget and I know all the locals. She's either a tourist or she's one of those mail order brides that keep popping up.

I stand there frozen in the shadows cast by the pine trees longer than I'd like to admit. Her freckles hold my attention, the way they cover her nose and most of her cheeks makes her look like a pixie. All she's missing are the wings.

She seems well prepared for her solo hike, and I feel awful for staring at her without announcing my presence. I doubt she would sing so boldly if she knew she wasn't alone. It takes effort to move my feet from where I've planted them as I watch her. I want to follow her and make sure she's safe, but she doesn't need me.

It's the thought of anger turning her pretty face mean that finally gets my feet moving away from the hiker. One step, then two more steps back into the shadows.

I'm about to turn around when I glance up the trail. I don't know if it's a slight movement that draws my attention or if it's just a twisting sensation in my gut that sets alarm bells ringing.

There is a mountain lion watching my hiker and judging by its posture the woman isn't going to be able to walk past unbothered.

Elizabeth

The roar catches me off guard just as I'm set to clear another rise on the trail. I glance behind me to see a fast-moving blur of hair and fur. Every instinct fails me as I neither fight nor flee. I freeze as a mountain of a man rushes past me.

His hair is wild and long just like his beard. Head to toe he is covered in fur and animals hides with a fierce expression of fury etched on his face.

"Fuck off you mangy cat!" I hear him yell.

His voice is deep and rough, catching in odd spots as he waves his arms at the mountain lion creeping down the trail. The cat is low to the ground, hissing and darting from side to side as the man continues to shout. I see rows of teeth that come to sharp points, and I want nothing more than to run back down the trail and get back in my van.

But the cat doesn't seem to be intimidated by the man's shouting or by his sheer size.

The man is easily six feet tall, and he has the bulk to match. The hides draped across his shoulders make him appear even larger. I watch the mountain lion continue its aggressive approach as a feeling of guilt sweeps over me. This man came out of the woods to save my life from a danger I wasn't even aware of and here I am wanting to run and leave him defenseless.

I can't leave him to deal with the cat by himself.

"Get back!" I shout at the lion.

The man's arms briefly pause as I add my voice to the verbal assault on the cat. It's the only acknowledgement that I receive as we continue to shout. I step out from behind the man to add my own arm motion.

Just a few feet from us the lion stops. Its eyes darting as both the man and I continue to shout and wave our arms. It's not very big. Certainly, smaller than a black bear. At this close range I can see its large teeth in clear detail as it hisses at us. I can see the fur that is puffing up to intimidate us, but we don't back down.

"Go away you ugly little fucker!" I shout in another bid to scare the cat.

Its ears flick toward me then flatten against its skull. I freeze as it bursts into motion, fearing the worst. But it doesn't charge me. It dashes left crashing through the shrubs that line the trail as it goes.

I take a breath preparing to thank the man who came to my rescue, but he beats me to the punch. Fury still etched into the fine lines of his forehead he redirects all the anger that he was throwing at the mountain lion at me, and I'm momentarily taken back.

"Are you trying to die?" he asks rhetorically. "Hiking alone is a good way to die a very painful and messy death."

He doesn't let me reply to his accusation as he continues ranting.

"That," he says pointing in the direction the mountain lion went. "Is the least of your worries. There are bears and wolves out here that would make a meal out of you in minutes. Not to mention dehydration or how easy it is to have a bad fall and risk a broken leg!"

"You're alone," I reply when he pauses for a breath.

This close I can see the broad ridge of his brow and the full lips outlined by his beard. He might be dressed like a bear, but this man is insanely gorgeous. Even if he's yelling at me like he thinks I'm stupid. I don't mention the water bottle that's clipped to my backpack. Or the bear mace that's on my keychain. It's not much but it's enough for a trail that sees plenty of foot traffic judging by how well-worn the path is under our boots.

"No bear spray that I can see," he adds unperturbed, and I nearly rattle my keychain in his face. "No gun or knife or any kind of defensive weapon! Do you not realize how often people get hurt on this trail? How many bear encounters we add to the national average? Are you trying to die?"

He pauses and looks at me expectantly. I remain silent as I stare into his dark green eyes. No. Hazel. The green shines so brightly in the sunshine I didn't notice the dark ring of brown that defines his irises.

"Of course not," I reply after a moment.

"You're just like all the other women who come here to find a husband before realizing how dangerous this mountain is."

I watch him glance to my left hand. He's searching for a wedding ring, I realize. I take the time to glance at his own hand and I'm pleased to note that his ring finger is also bare.

"Go back to where you came from," he bites out. "A beautiful woman like you doesn't belong out here."

Reeling from him calling me beautiful it takes me a minute to realize he's heading back off the trail. After railing at me about how defenseless and unsuited I am to the terrain and wildlife the lout is just going to abandon me.

"My name is Elizabeth," I call after the man, hoping he'll give me his name in return.

His silence irks me especially when he points at the trail indicating I should go back to my van.

"Thanks for your help!" I add. "You're my hero!"

My voice is loud and filled with cheer. He might be a grumpy grouch, but he did save my life. In a world where no one will hesitate to whip out a phone and record injustice rather than intervene and help, he stepped forward.

I don't care that he's covered in dirt and wearing animal skins. As I head back down the trail to my van, I feel lighter than the high altitude air. I didn't make it to the overlook, but I found something better.

I've finally found a man who catches my eye. And despite not knowing his name, I already know that I've picked the perfect man. He might be grumpy and rough around the edges, but he didn't hesitate to protect a stranger. He called me beautiful like it was an insult rather than a compliment. He's not going to spew flowery words to seduce me.

If anything, I suspect it'll be me who will have to talk my way into his bed. But first I need to gather some intel, like his name among other details. Lucky me, I know just who to ask.

Jeb

I had to force myself to walk away from the hiker. Elizabeth. Brave and fearless she stood next to me helping to scare the mountain lion away. And then she turned those big blue eyes on me and for a moment I was struck senseless. She looked up at me with so much trust and all I wanted to do was throw her over my shoulder and carry her off to my cabin.

The possessive need to make her mine was overwhelming and shocking. I might live off grid, but I've always considered myself civilized. I help the fire and rescue department from time to time by finding lost hikers. I repaint trail signs and keep an eye out for poaching for the rangers. I prefer my isolation, but I have manners, and I like contributing to the community.

Which is why I'm deeply ashamed of how I yelled at her.

Elizabeth.

The name doesn't fit her. It's such a stern name for such a pretty flower. Her frame so delicate like a stem and her eyes the exact shade of blue as delphiniums. A rare flower to be found in our mountains but the color pops amongst the green and brown of the forest floor when they grow. A woman as pretty as a flower deserves a name just as delicate and pretty. Already I've given her a nickname. In my mind she'll always be Ellie. Pretty and cute just like my hiker.

And that's why I need to stay away from her. She didn't seem to be bothered by my yelling or my tone but that's no excuse. She's not in Crescent Ridge for me. As pretty as she is I have no doubt she came here through that mail order bride program.

I'm tempted to go down to town just to find the slouch she's going to marry and give him an earful. None of my friends would have let their brides go on that trail alone. There are too many risks.

A few days later just as I'm weighing a trip down to the fire station to visit my buddy Shawn, I get a visitor.

Not in the traditional sense. She doesn't come up to the cabin or approach me as I go about my day. She lingers in the woods as I chop firewood and she follows at a distance as I check my traps. I should be furious that she's spying on me. Furious that she came up this mountain alone a second time. Instead, I find myself slowing my steps so she can keep pace. I take easier trails when I go out and spend more time in my garden than ever before so she can rest.

After the first day I expect her to lose interest. Whatever curiosity she had is surely sated. I love my life and the way I live, but visually I'm certain it must be boring to watch.

Day after day she comes back. Each time I spot her without her realizing. The few times she doesn't show up by noon I venture down to town. The first time I didn't have a shadow I had to break out the razor. If I wanted to find my flower, I needed to blend in. With a shave and a small haircut paired with a flannel shirt and denim jeans I fit in better in town than she did in the brush. She never noticed me following her, but I did get some odd looks from Mama Mary and Shawn.

The three days she couldn't make it up the mountain and I went to her is two more times I've been in town than all last year.

She's not losing interest I realize one day when I stop to bathe in the river. The water is cold but it's not the temperature that has the hairs on my arms rising. It's her.

I can feel those baby blue eyes on me like a physical touch.

Despite the chilly air and the icy water, I feel myself getting hard at the thought of Ellie watching me bathe. I felt her eyes on me the entire time as I stripped out of my clothing. She didn't look away. Even when I slid my pants down, exposing my cock to her gaze. I know exactly which tree she's lurking behind and I made sure to give her time to look.

If these past few days weren't an invasion of privacy, *this* certainly is.

Any residual guilt I felt for those few stolen moments before I spotted that mountain lion is long gone. Of the two of us, only one is truly a stalker.

If my flower wants a show, she'll get one.

I climb out of the water and lay on a large rock in the sun. The heavy shaft of my cock slapping against my stomach as I lay down. I can see her in my peripheral vision, crouched by a tree and partially hidden by some shrubs. She's done better with her outfit today, wearing a green tank top and dark brown pants. If she really wants to blend in though she needs to hide more of her skin. Her arms are tan but not dark enough to prevent her from standing out in the brush.

My hand feels cold as it strokes my cock. Nothing like how her warm little mouth would feel. Keeping my attention on her I hear her gasp as I stroke my palm over the head. She's quick to muffle it but she doesn't look away.

As I continue to stroke my cock, I imagine how this would play out if she were to step out and announce her presence. Would she sink to her knees and take me in her mouth? Or would she climb on top of me and use me to find her own pleasure?

At the thought of her bouncing on me, her small breasts lifting and falling with the motion of her hips I feel the tingle at the base of my spine. My balls grow tight, and I come in a long spurt across my stomach.

A waste. So many other places I would rather see it drip from.

For a single moment I can't help myself. I turn my head and look to where Ellie is hiding. I let my eyes find hers and I see the moment she realizes I know she's there. Her blue eyes are wide with fright. Relaxed from my release I find myself smiling at her.

Sliding back into the water I wash off the seed that is still warm on my skin. I hear a branch snap but don't look as I hear the soft footsteps of my hiker disappearing further into the forest.

Dressing in a hurry I can't let her get too far out of my sight. Each day that she's left after following me I return the favor and accompany her down the mountain. Ellie's never been aware of my presence, but I've been there, nonetheless. I wasn't joking about the bears. I follow her trail for a few feet before I hear a startled yelp.

She's not screaming and judging by the location of her shout I know exactly what caused that reaction.

Elizabeth

"**F**uck!" I shout once I hit the ground.

Wrapped around my leg is a piece of wire that doesn't belong in nature. The wire has turned my ankle red but aside from the fall I'm fine. Some light scrapes on my palms from where they struck rocks as I tried to catch myself from face planting into the rocky soil. I've followed Jeb for the better part of a week, and I should know where his traps are by now. I've seen him check them every day I've been up here.

The only days I didn't make it up the mountain to stalk him were the days I had shifts scheduled at the diner. During one of which I was able to interrogate Mama Mary about the reclusive mountain man who looks more like a bear than a man. And she was only too happy to sing his praises. Seems mister bear is an unofficial member of fire and rescue. And an honorary forest ranger.

I sit up just in time to see a large shadow fall over me blocking out the midday sun overhead.

"Look what I've caught," his deep voice rumbles above me and I fight the urge to duck my head and avoid his gaze.

His feet are bare beside my own, he must have skipped his boots when he got dressed to chase after me. I know he saw me. Looking up I see his bare chest dusted with dark hair looming above me. Gaze riveted, I see water droplets running down his warm tan skin as my mouth goes dry.

"Miracle, you haven't landed in one of my traps sooner," he says as his hands go to the wire tangled around my ankle. "With the way you've been traipsing all over this mountain you were overdue to be caught."

"You knew I was watching," I mutter.

Another woman might be embarrassed to be caught ogling a man bathing in the river. Or to have followed him for the last week. I only ran because I didn't know what else to do. Now I'm caught red handed without the decency to blush.

"No, frigid dips in the river turn me on," he says with a chuckle that has me wetter than the river he bathed in. "Of course I knew you were there. You're not the most subtle."

"You should have said something," I gripe as his hands work quickly to get my foot free of the trap.

"I thought my method was more effective," he says as his hand runs up my calf.

If there wasn't a layer of nylon between our skin, I would be melting into a puddle at his feet. He takes my hands in his as he stands and uses his grip to help me to my feet.

Before I can find my footing, he's released my hands and dipped down in front of me. Without a word the man grabs the back of my thighs as he hauls me over his shoulder. A second later and I'm staring at the ground and his ass.

"I can walk," I say as I pat his back to get his attention.

I try as hard as I can not to notice the delicious way that his warm wet skin feels beneath my palms.

"I'm faster and I know where all the traps are," he replies.

He carries me through the woods with a brief stop to gather his clothes that he left on the riverbank. Not once does he put me down, no matter how much I protest. Nor does he put his boots on. He walks barefoot across the rocky ground without a wince, whereas my feet are sore from the week of hiking in the most comfortable boots I could find.

"It's not that weird, right?" I ask once I realize he's serious about carrying me the entire way to his cabin. "I mean I needed to know you weren't *weird*."

Jeb is silent through the walk as I ramble on about my behavior this past week. My father was a lawyer, and I know if I keep talking long enough, I'll come up with an argument that sounds logical.

"I love your home," I gush as he walks up the well-worn path that leads to his cabin. "But you need to get chickens. They're so cute and they lay eggs! One less thing you need to get from town."

"I'm not getting chickens, Ellie," he mutters as he carries me through his garden gate. "I'd just be feeding the predators. Like your friend, the mountain lion."

"That's why you build a coop with a strong fence around it," I argue.

"Still would act as a lure, bringing bears and wolves closer to the cabin," he retorts as he takes us across his porch.

Jeb's stride eats up the long wooden planked distance in half the time it would take me to do the same.

"You should get a couple of rocking chairs for this porch," I tell him. "The view from here is gorgeous."

Once inside he sets me down and leaves me standing in the center of a living room bigger than any apartment, I've ever lived in. His walls have wood paneling and with the buffalo plaid blankets draped across his couch and the mounted deer heads on his walls his cabin looks like a hunter's cabin straight out of the movies.

"It's a little rustic," Jeb says with a sheepish expression as he disappears into his kitchen.

"I don't care," I call after him. "I love it!"

"Solar power that never fully charges anything and a well that always runs muddy when it rains," he replies as he comes back out carrying two glasses of water. "Not exactly what every woman dreams of."

I take a glass from him, taking a small sip of the cold water.

"Good," I reply before sitting down on his couch. "Less competition."

I watch as he chokes on his sip of water. His booming coughs echo around the room as I take another drink of water to hide my smirk.

"Besides, it has more space than my van," I add.

"Hard not to," Jeb mutters.

"I swear my apartment is smaller," I say pressing a hand over my heart in a solemn vow. "The only upside about that place is the bathroom. Do you know how many outdoor showers I've taken that I've had to cut short because of guys trying to sneak a peek?"

His answering growl takes me by surprise. I shouldn't feel a sliver of pleasure at the possessive sound, but it warms my body down to my toes.

"Traveling as a single woman can be dangerous. You talk about the bears and wolves but I'm more worried about the men."

The frown that tightens the corner of his lips isn't possessive or jealous. It's difficult to read. Almost like, he's guilty?

"If you want to go down the mountain today, so that you're not alone-" his voice cracks cutting off his words but his last words though unspoken are the loudest of all.

with me.

"No," I say with a harshness that shocks even me. "I'm fine with you. Staying with you. Alone."

I could curse my awkwardness. The stumbling and halting pattern of my words only makes the conversation worse. If he thinks I'm afraid of him, he's wrong. I've never felt safer.

"Okay," he says with his earlier frown melting into a smile that sends heat rushing to my core. "Then you'll stay."

Jeb

"Why do you keep your pans here?" Ellie asks from where she is rearranging the kitchen.

A shrug is my only answer as she empties the contents of another cabinet. The entire contents of my kitchen are covering the counters. Glassware, plates, bowls, and pans litter every surface available.

"Miracle you can find anything," she mutters to herself as she begins putting items away.

I don't think there was a problem with where things were, but Ellie was bothered. She's rearranging my kitchen even though she is not staying. No matter that I said the complete opposite an hour ago.

She can't stay.

She has an entire life down in town. She has friends and a job. She has carved out a place for herself in Crescent

Ridge. Ellie deserves better than an off-grid cabin with a man who resembles a bear.

She deserves the world. A big house and a loving husband and a family who would appreciate her warm and carefree nature.

"Do you need two skillets?" she asks, pulling me from my thoughts.

"One came with a set and the other I bought because the first one sucked."

"You should have tossed one," Ellie scolds. "That's exactly how you end up with clutter."

"Can't wait to see what you do with the bedroom," I say before I think of the implication of my words.

"Hopefully it's in a better state than this trainwreck," she mutters.

"Same guy decorated it," I say with a laugh. "Heard he doesn't have a degree in interior design, the slob."

"You're not a slob," Ellie replies. "Just unorganized."

I watch as she moves around my kitchen, organizing it to suit her needs and I have to admit that she looks good in my home. I can see her swollen with our child as she makes us dinner. I can imagine her decorating my drab house and insisting we need new drapes when our old ones are perfectly fine.

Ellie is my every desire come to life, but I know the hardships that come with this life. Miles away from the closest hospital, even a good hike from the nearest EMT, in a medical emergency it would be difficult to find help. I've had to treat my own gunshot wound when a poacher mistook me for a bear. If Ellie were hurt, I don't know if I could get her down the mountain in time.

She deserves better.

It's getting late and I'm not sold that her ankle isn't sprained. She'll spend the night and in the morning I'll escort her down to Crescent Ridge.

I follow her to the bedroom fully prepared for her to criticize everything from the color to the furniture placement. I'm not going to tell her that the kitchen already looks better thanks to her meddling.

Elizabeth

"Ellie what are you doing?" Jeb asks from the doorway.

I look up from where I am undressing to see his eyes locked on my bare skin. I'm not completely naked. I still have on a shirt and my underwear. But by the heated look in his eyes, I might as well be wearing nothing at all.

"Getting ready for bed?" I reply, curious as to why he looks so startled.

"I'll just-" he begins before choking on his next words. "I'll be on the couch."

"No." I reply just barely resisting the urge to stomp my foot on the hardwood floor. "You will not."

"Ellie." he says looking at my feet as he audibly swallows. "I can't. I can't be in the same room with you when you look like that."

I glance down at my body, insecurity flaring to life before I shake it off. I know this man and I know he's just trying to do what he thinks is right. He thinks I'm some flighty creature that's going to spend the night in his bed and then traipse down the mountains in the morning never to be seen again.

But I'm not. I'm not going anywhere. And if he won't listen to the words then I'll show him with my actions.

I'm done arguing with him. Instead, I reach for the hem of my T-shirt, where it hangs just above my knees, and in one fluid move I whip it over my head and toss it to the ground at his feet.

His dark gaze snaps to mine like an elastic band pulled too tight. He is across the room wrapping his arms around me before I can get the band of my bra undone. The rough calluses on his fingers scrape the tender skin at my waist where he grabs me, but I don't care. I love that he's made a life for himself out here. That his body shows signs of the effort that took only makes my body burn hotter.

His kiss Is unlike anything else I've ever experienced. The pressure is gentle, but his passion turns our kiss frenzied. His hands go to my ass and my hands tangle in his long hair the strands wrapping around my fingers as we fight to get closer.

When I pull back to catch my breath all I see is heat and desire in his expression. He's done fighting this. He was done when he climbed into that stream today. I'm sure he'll deny it but we both know that this isn't a momentary attraction. This is love. This is forever.

We don't speak as we move towards the bed his hands on my body the entire time. Everywhere his hands touch me sets my body on fire. My skin is tingling and the tension that has been building between us is cresting into a wave of heated desire.

"Ellie," he groans as I fall back onto the bed.

"Not getting any younger," I taunt as I slip my bra and panties off.

Jeb stands at the foot of the bed watching as I strip. His eyes burn a path from my pink tipped breasts down to the apex of my thighs.

His knees hit the floor with a thud before he reaches out to grab my legs, pulling me to the edge of the bed. My thighs land on his shoulders a second before his mouth finds my core.

Long licks tease me as I twist my hands into the navy sheets. I open my eyes to glare at the scratchy material, my focus pulled away from the man between my legs.

"Stop thinking about the sheets," Jeb pulls back to say.

"I can't help it!" I giggle. "They're hideous."

"If your mind is anywhere else but right here then I'm not doing a good enough job," he growls.

His fingers spread open my folds leaving my clit bare to his tongue. The first touch of his tongue to the sensitive bundle of nerves has me arching off the bed. I feel more than hear the deep rumble of his chuckle as he builds a steady rhythm.

Fire burns through my veins as I come in a rush, my arousal coating Jeb's mouth. My core clenches, the muscles flexing on nothing, leaving me feeling hollow and empty. He licks me through my orgasm, the sounds his mouth makes obscene, unbothered by my legs squeezing his head like a vice.

"Let me in, Ellie," Jeb murmurs as he climbs up to kneel on the bed between my legs.

He's slipped out of his clothes while I've laid boneless in his bed, coming back down to earth.

Wordlessly I wrap my arms around his neck, letting my thighs fall open to make room for him.

"Still with me?" he whispers into my ear as he notches the head of his cock at my entrance.

"Yes," I whimper. "Hurry Jeb."

"Eager little thing," he murmurs as he begins pushing his way inside me. "We're not rushing this."

His cock is long and thick with a mushroom shaped head and dark veins running down the length. Halfway in he stops and gives me time to adjust to his size despite how wet I am.

"More," I order causing him to huff a laugh.

"Not. Rushing," he bites out with two well timed thrusts punctuating the words.

I would laugh at his stubbornness but I'm too busy stroking every inch of skin I can reach. His hard pectorals, the sinewy muscles of his arms, everything I can touch, I grab, squeeze, and fondle.

It's when I lean up and bite his left nipple with more force than play that his control snaps.

His breath is heavy in my ear as he grabs my thighs, each hand gripping tightly, and holds me in place as he begins fucking me in earnest.

"So fucking bossy," he growls as he uses his weight to pin me to the bed beneath him. "Just can't enjoy a gentle moment with you."

"Gentle? More like slow," I throw back.

My sass makes his eyes glint in the shadows. With my next breath Jeb uses his grip on my thighs to bring my feet together and push them towards my chest. His next thrust hits so deep it has me seeing stars.

"So good little flower," he growls above me.

Every pounding press of his hips to mine only adds to the heat building and turning molten inside my core. I fall apart with his name on my lips, his roar shattering the stillness around us a moment later. The warmth of his seed splashing my inner walls as my legs slump onto the bed as Jeb releases his hold on my thighs.

I tug Jeb down until he relaxes his weight, covering my body with his like a warm weighted blanket. We lie together until sleep is beginning to drag me under when Jeb startles awake.

"Hang on," he mumbles as he pulls away.

His cock hangs heavy between his thighs, shiny with our combined release, as he goes to fetch a wet cloth. With an unexpected gentleness he cleans us both before he climbs into bed beside me.

"Cold," I grumble snuggling into his side as he huffs a laugh.

The blanket he drags over our naked bodies is worn with use but soft as a cloud. Between the blankets and his body heat I return to my previous state of boneless bliss. At this rate, the mattress will absorb me, my limbs heavy with exhaustion. I mean to talk to him, talk about us and how we'll make this work, but I fall asleep moments after his arms wrap around me.

Jeb

Waking up late with the sunlight filtering through the white linen curtains, that Ellie called basic, I stretch out and all I find is empty space beside me. For a moment I think Ellie has left me. That she's gone down the mountain in the early light of day to avoid an awkward morning conversation.

Then I hear the scraping of a chair dragging along the hardwood floor and I know that she's still here. I wouldn't stop her from leaving if she wanted to return to her old life. But if she wants to stay then I will be the happiest man on this mountain.

I spot my pants on the floor, but I can't find my shirt. I settle for the pants as I go to find my woman.

"What you got there Ellie?" I ask as I come into the kitchen.

She's leaning over the kitchen table dressed in nothing but my shirt and she's writing on a scrap piece of paper with a pen.

"To do list," she replies writing something else down.

I walk up behind her and peer over her shoulder to see the list she's made.

Pack

Give Notice at Lenny's

Setup P.O. Box

I snort as I pluck the pen from her hand and scratch off the last item on her list.

"Don't need two, I already got one."

Ellie giggles and emboldened I add one more thing to her list. The most important of the three. My hand shakes as I write the two words.

Get Married

Ellie's shoulders tense under my palms as she reads what I've written. Her head tilts to the side and her blue eyes peer up at me through her dark eyelashes. I can see the question floating in her eyes. I tried to be nonchalant, but I know she needs the words.

She deserves the words.

I sink down to kneel beside her.

"I don't have a ring," I tell her. "I wasn't prepared to meet the woman of my dreams in the middle of nowhere. You deserve more than what I can offer but I'll provide for you and our family. I will love you through easy times and hard until I take my last breath."

Ellie's eyes shine with unshed tears as she takes in my words.

"Will you marry me?" I ask her biting back tears of my own.

"Of course I will," she says as she loops her arms around my neck.

I go to stand at the same time that she surges forward for a hug and we both tumble to the floor in a tangle of limbs.

"I love you too," she whispers into my ear.

My heart thuds heavily in my chest. Her words send me soaring higher than the peak of the mountain we live on.

"My lovely little flower," I whisper as I crush her against my chest. "You belong to the mountain just as much as I do."

"Always."

Epilogue

Elizabeth

O ne Year Later

"Finally got the satellite phone set up," Jeb says from where he is seated in his rocking chair on the porch beside me.

"Perfect," I say as I rock back and forth.

Knitting isn't the easiest hobby to master but I still have four months before the baby is due to work on this blanket I'm making for him. I'm making a blue and white merino wool baby blanket in my spare time, while Jeb preps the house for our winter arrival.

"We'll be down in town before it starts snowing," Jeb reassures me for the hundredth time.

Once we realized we were pregnant, and the baby would be due in the colder months Jeb started panicking. He worried and stressed himself over the logistics of the delivery until I suggested renting an apartment for the winter.

No need to make our way down the mountain in the snow and ice while I'm in labor. We'll be closer to the local doctor and the clinic and the hospital down in Bramble if things take a bad turn.

For how much we prefer our privacy on our own slice of the mountain we both agreed to live in town from the beginning of winter until I give birth.

"Crib is set up," Jeb says as he eases back into his chair.

"My blanket is a work in progress," I say holding up the rows I've knitted.

I omit that Lily started the project for me. I was never going to figure it out without help. On her fourth baby she has made blankets for each without help and she was the ideal person to ask for assistance.

"You don't need to worry about making anything other than our little peanut," Jeb says, reaching over to take my hand.

"It's just a blanket," I reply.

"Baby and blanket," he says with a firm nod. "Nothing else."

"If I finish this early enough, I'm making booties," I say.

I watch him glance at the pile of loose yarn in my lap with a skeptical expression. I swat at his arm as he bursts into laughter before I join him.

"Shut your mouth," I say between gasping breaths.

"I didn't say anything," he protests.

"Your eyes said enough," I reply.

"Eyes can't talk," he argues.

"Yours did."

"Did they?" he asks. "Bad eyes."

His eyes drop to my breasts with obvious heat. More like naughty eyes.

"Have I told you that you are the most gorgeous woman I have ever seen?"

"Not today."

"You," he says before pressing a soft kiss to my lips. "Are the hottest woman I have ever seen."

"Don't see many women around these parts," I tease even as I drop my pile of tangled yarn into the basket beside my feet.

"Only woman I need is you," Jeb growls. "My perfect flower."

I sway my hips as I lead the way into the house. We're isolated enough but it only took one hiker spotting us mid-orgasm in the river to have me shying away from outdoor sex.

"No other woman is going to stalk you," I say as I reach for the zipper on the back of my dress.

"I'm not shaving for anyone else." Jeb's words warm my body even as his breath hits my neck sending chills down my spine.

My arms break out in gooseflesh as his lips find my neck. His kisses are teasingly light as he makes his way to my shoulder, pushing the strap of my dress down my arm as he goes. With my baby bump dresses have become my favorite clothing choice. I don't feel like fighting leggings every morning because my pants no longer button.

"No one else is getting me into fancy shirts."

His lips leave my skin long enough to finish tugging off my dress.

"Flannel is *not* fancy," I protest.

His mouth finds my sensitive nipples and my core drips with every flick of his tongue. It's like there is a live wire strung between my nipples and my clit. Every touch of his teeth and tongue sends electrical pulses directly to my pussy.

"I'll wear whatever you want," he growls against my breast. "I'll go wherever you want. Pack up the van and tour the country. Visit every fucking city so long as you let me do this every day."

"Not a chance in hell," I mutter as he gently tips me back onto the bed. "We'll spend the winter in town just to be safe and then we're coming right back home."

"As you wish," Jeb says before he leans down to kiss me.

Our mouths move in a familiar rhythm, one we've perfected over time. My husband moves over my body like a thunderstorm, all loud rumbles, and tingling shocks as he works me into a frenzy.

"Ellie," he pants when I grab his cock. "Not now. I'm too worked up from watching you prance around in that dress."

"Hmm," I reply noncommittedly as I stroke my hand up and down his length in a smooth glide.

Jeb's hands clench the bedsheets on either side of my head, his forearms straining as he tries to fight back his orgasm. Just as he's about to explode, he jerks his hips back pulling his cock out of my reach.

"I'm not finishing in your hand," he growls.

I'm tempted to sink down and take him in my mouth but judging by how dark his hazel eyes have gotten there is only one place he plans to put his cock. The same place I'm desperate to feel his touch.

His grip on my hips is firm but not bruising as he pushes his cock into me. Ever since the positive pregnancy test, he's been absurdly gentle. No matter how I push him to be more aggressive and demanding.

"Hurry or I'll finish without you," I tell him with a playful smirk.

I reach for my clit, intent on rubbing myself closer to orgasm but I never make it that far. Jeb grabs my hand and forces it above my head. Arching into him the tips of my breasts brush his chest, the sensitive flesh scratched by his coarse chest hair.

"Always in a rush," he grumbles as he sets a brutal pace.

Every thrust brings his pelvis in line with my clit, each bump sending me higher. I love it when he gets bossy. When I can tease and torment him until he snaps and lets his control slip. Ever the loving husband when he fucks me, he becomes animalistic in his drive. The sounds of our bodies meeting are obscene in the quiet of the cabin. Flesh slapping against flesh with the wet squelch of my muscles milking his cock with every withdrawal.

"Jeb," I cry coming apart in his arms just before his hips falter.

"Ellie," he groans in my ear as my muscles clamp down on him.

His cock pulses as the warmth of his seed coats my walls.

"I love you," I tell him later as we lie in bed with the ivory white sheets tangled around us.

"I love you more," he replies without hesitating. "And I love our baby."

I never knew where I would end up when I started traveling in my van. I wanted to see as much of the world as I could, to gain life experiences, and to find some understanding about life. What I found on that hiking trail all those months ago tops everything I thought I would find. Love and desire with the one person who sees me just as I am.

When Jeb says sweet nothings, they're not nothings. He says what he means and means what he says. I couldn't ask for a better man to be my husband and as he strokes a calloused palm over the bump where our baby grows, I know I couldn't find a better father for our child.

I found love on this mountain and there is nowhere else I would rather be.

The End

Liam has found the woman meant to be his. There's just one teeny tiny problem. She's in Crescent Ridge as a mail order bride, just not his. Can Liam stop the wedding and convince Alisa to swap grooms? Find out in Mountain Man's Stolen Mail Order Bride.

You can sign up for my newsletter or follow me on Amazon to stay up to date on new releases.

Mountain Man's Stolen Mail Order Bride

Jacqueline Carmine

Alisa

S omething is not right.

My friends told me I was going all in too soon. I should have listened to them, but I wanted to take a chance on love for the first time in my life. I always wanted to find true love but didn't take the time to do anything about it. Work kept me busy, and I never tried too hard to look for Mr. Right.

Being thirty and unmarried I didn't want to go bar hopping or clubbing. I didn't want to waste my time on a man who wasn't ready for forever. The mail order bride program seemed like the answer. Everyone on the site was verified and all were looking for the same thing. Someone to spend forever with.

Marrying a man I barely know didn't seem so crazy a week ago. My parents knew each other for years before they married, and their love still died.

Now I'm standing in the church where we're set to be married this afternoon. I'm in my wedding dress and my hair and makeup are done. When I finished planning this event, I wanted it all to go smoothly. I was going to be ready early and walk down the aisle on time. Now I'm paying for that over-the-top planning by shuffling into the church in a mass of tulle and lace that makes every movement awkward.

I can't do it.

He's supposed to be getting the church ready with his groomsmen. I don't see the other men, nor do I see any of the flowers I picked out. The church doesn't look any different than it would for a Sunday service.

It's another strike against my fiancé. I've taken our wedding and future marriage seriously, but he has treated the entire affair like a second thought. Now that I'm standing in the church with cold feet, I wonder why he hasn't already called the wedding off.

Reasons are piling up for why this was a horrible idea to get married so quickly. He doesn't want to marry me any more than I want to marry him.

Tyler's car was in the parking lot, so I know he's around here somewhere. Probably for the best that he's alone. This conversation will be easier without an audience.

He's part of a traveling construction crew that is stationed in Crescent Ridge for the next month finishing up a new bistro. That's part of why I'm getting cold feet. We haven't lived together yet or even had sex but by marrying him I'm signing up to travel the country with no real roots.

After my parent's divorce I've craved stability. And Crescent Ridge already feels like home.

I walk down the aisle mourning the fact that I won't be getting the wedding of my dreams. At least not today. Another reason this was a bad idea. I was looking forward to my dream wedding with more enthusiasm than life with Tyler afterward.

There is a room off to the side of the altar, where I can only assume Tyler is at least putting on his tuxedo. As I get closer to the wooden door I hear the muffled sound of voices. Maybe he does have a few of his groomsmen with him. They could have driven over together in his car.

Just as I go to knock in case they're all changing clothes, I hear a loud feminine moan. My hand freezes just shy of the door. My eyes close as I listen to the obvious sounds of sex on the other side of the door. The moans, the sound of skin slapping against skin, and the creaking of furniture are all dead giveaways.

I wait for a moment but the sadness I expected doesn't come. No tears to shed for the man I was set to marry this afternoon. I consider leaving but I don't want to put off this conversation for later. Our ceremony is less than two hours away and I need to make several phone calls to cancel the entire production.

No, I can't put this off.

Besides, I'm curious to see who he's fucking on what was meant to be our wedding day. I might not be sad, but I do feel a burst of anger at the blatant display of disrespect.

I test the doorknob and find it unlocked. The door swings open with a loud creak but the couple having sex on the bench don't notice. Tyler's jeans and boxers are around his ankles and he's still wearing a shirt. The woman who is bent over the bench, ass in the air is completely naked. Her dress is on the floor beside Tyler's feet.

Her purple fucking dress. I watch in shock as Tyler's hands wrap themselves in her brown curly hair. Just like mine. He yanks hard and her neck arches until I can see her face.

Her brown eyes open just in time to meet mine before I start screaming.

"You're fucking my *mom*?" I scream at the top of my lungs.

Tyler trips over his jeans as he whirls around to see me. His face is as pale as his ass and his dick, which is quickly going soft, is smaller than he claimed. My mother scrambles for her dress as Tyler hits his knees as he continues to fumble with his pants.

"Are you serious?" I continue to scream. "My mom? Of all the women you could have picked, you cheat with my mother?"

"Honey," my mother says as she clutches her dress to her chest. "It was an accident."

Tyler finally able to find his feet and get his pants pulled up, turns to look at my mother in irritation, completely disregarding my presence.

"You accidentally fucked me five times?" he shouts at my mother.

The sarcasm in his voice is the last straw for my frazzled mother.

"It was a *fling,* you moron," she shouts back. "You are marrying my daughter."

"Not anymore!" I shout to be heard over the yelling pair.

My words are ignored.

"This," My mother says as she waves a hand between Tyler and herself. "was an itch I needed scratched."

Finally turning to look at me, my mother adopts a soft smile.

"I understand you're upset, Alisa," she says as she steps towards me. "But this will all be ancient history soon enough."

Matching every step she takes towards me with a step backward I maintain the distance between us.

"I am not marrying him," I tell my mother.

Tyler is a worthless cheating prick, but I don't love him. His betrayal doesn't hurt like it should. But hers cuts deep.

"Don't be ridiculous," my mother replies. "This is your wedding day!"

"No, it's not," I say before I turn my back on the pair of them and storm my way back up the aisle.

I walked into this church expecting to end one relationship. Now I have the wreckage of two behind me and the path forward is more of a blur than ever.

Liam

Thirty-one years old and I've never made a fool of myself over a woman. Until now. I don't know what it is about the brunette that has me tripping over myself trying to gather the courage to approach her.

I saw her on Main Street outside the flower shop laughing at something that Mrs. Clarke said. Her bubbly laugh caught my attention from a block away pulling me from a conversation with William about a rocking chair he wants me to make for his wife.

"Liam?" His voice sounded far away as I stared down the street at the woman.

I'll never forget the first time I saw her. The smile on her face raising her blushing cheeks. Her hazel eyes shimmering in the sunlight as she stood next to the florist. Even in flats she towered over Mrs. Clarke.

The yellow sundress that fluttered in the wind had a halter top that showed off her freckled shoulders and her brown hair was pulled up high letting her curls barely brush her skin.

It took three more attempts on William's part to drag my attention away from her. And even then, I was in denial about her effect on me. Throughout the week I caught sight of her as she planned her wedding.

The most stunning woman I've ever seen, and someone had already put a ring on her finger. Even knowing that she was spoken for I couldn't help myself. The town was abuzz with the news of her wedding to one of the construction workers. Even if I didn't seek out every drop of information about her I could, I still would have known today was her wedding.

The local inn is filled with friends and family attending the wedding, and most of the locals have been offered an invitation as well. Even Barb and Betty Anderson are invited. If I had stopped to talk to her outside that flower shop or anywhere else this week, I probably would have received an invite too.

And I can't sit idly by while she marries another man. I know it's insane, but I can't help it. I need her to see me. If she still wants to marry her fiancé after she meets me, I don't know what I'll do.

I'm climbing up the steps to the church where she's set to be married when the double oak doors slam open. She's the topper of a white cloud as she storms out of the church with a venomous glare aimed at the ground. Her forehead scrunched into tiny white lines.

"Going somewhere in a hurry, gorgeous?" I ask before I can filter my words.

She comes to an abrupt stop in front of me. Her frown melts just a tad as her hazel eyes meet mine. I stuff my hands into the front pockets of my jeans to prevent myself from reaching out to touch her. This is the closest the two of us have ever been and I'm struggling not to reach for her.

To see if her skin is as soft as it looks. If her curls are springy or loose when tugged. She glances behind me, and when I turn to look, all I see is the nearly empty parking lot that only has one car besides my truck.

"I need to get out of here," she pleads with her eyes turning glassy with unshed tears.

Without a word I turn on my heel and offer her my arm. My breath catches in my throat when she loops her own through it without hesitation. She's pressed up close to me and I can't think straight let alone speak as we walk back to my truck. The skirt of her dress is poufy, and it crumples between our legs as we walk.

She doesn't say a word until she's in the truck and I'm starting to close her door.

"Alisa," she says and despite it being the most basic communication possible it takes me a moment to give her my name in return.

"Liam," I say after a long pause. "I'll get you out of here."

Alisa

I didn't have a plan when I stormed out of the church. I couldn't fit my dress in my mother's car, so I walked over from the nearby inn where I got ready. I can't go back to the inn because that's where my mother is staying, and she has a key to my room. Not a keycard, an old-fashioned skeleton key. I was planning to travel with Tyler after the wedding, so I sold my car before I came out here.

The helplessness I feel only adds to my anger. I'm at the mercy of a stranger. A man I only know from local gossip. Even if he hadn't told me his name, I would know who he is. In a small town it's impossible to be anonymous. He might be a stranger, but I know a lot about the man who is driving me away from the trainwreck of my life.

He's a volunteer firefighter who specializes in wood-working and is loved by everyone in Crescent Ridge. I've seen him around town as I planned my wedding. It's hard not to stick out when you have a body like his. He's an inch or two shorter than me but he has muscles on top of muscles.

I might have ogled him more than an engaged woman should have. Crescent Ridge is bursting with men, most of them attractive enough to be on a smutty book cover but Liam is on another level. From his honey blonde hair to his barrel chest the man is a walking wet dream.

If I wasn't engaged, I would have tried to flirt my way into his bed.

He drives us out of town, and I spend the drive sneaking covert glances at him. I should get him to stop by the inn so that I can grab my stuff, but I don't want to run into a nosy local. As much as I love the small mountain town I'm beginning to see the downside. My cancelled wedding is going to draw a lot of attention. I would have to be a fool to think otherwise. But I don't need to parade myself in front of them like a sideshow attraction.

We're turning up a winding gravel road when my phone starts to ring. Startled, it takes me more than a minute to wrangle it free from the confines of my corset top.

I see my mother's name and photo and immediately disconnect the call. I swipe over to my messaging app and send a text to my friends in the group chat.

Wedding off, caught Tyler banging my mom in the church. Going dark.

I don't want anyone showing up to the church expecting to see me walk down the aisle. It's a no brainer to power off my phone immediately after. I don't want to speak to my mother or Tyler for the foreseeable future. Or to answer the interrogation my friends are surely planning. Let them ask my mother all the pertinent questions.

Liam parks his truck in front of an A-frame cabin that has a wooden porch with a railing that is carved to look like branches. It has a rustic appeal, and it blends in well with the pine trees surrounding it.

It suits him.

"I'll get some clothes you can change into," Liam says when he opens my door.

I follow him up the steps to the cabin, my eyes on the muscles straining against the fabric of his red flannel the entire time. He disappears into a bedroom, leaving me in a living room decorated with cool blue and green tones. They say men have no taste in décor, but I'd have to say that his cabin looks better than my apartment.

Now with everything I own packed into a moving van it's no contest. I'm absolutely one hundred percent jealous of his magazine worthy home.

"Here," Liam says handing me a T-shirt and a comfortable looking pair of sweatpants.

"Thanks," I reply.

Fifteen minutes later according to the wall clock in his bathroom and I'm no closer to getting out of my wedding dress. It's a corset top laced up in the back with a ballgown skirt.

And I can barely reach the laces. Every tug only seems to tie the knot of the bow tighter. It hurts my pride a bit, but I find myself wandering back into Liam's living room to seek his help.

"Changed your mind about the wedding?" he asks, looking up from the open tackle box sitting on his coffee table.

"No!" I reply with venom. "Never."

His eyebrows raise at my tone, but I watch his blue eyes grow heated as they rake down my body, shivers following their path. For a moment I let myself forget that I'm wearing a wedding dress I bought to marry another man. For just a moment I feel like a bride.

Liam's eyes dart back to mine and while I expect to see him look ashamed of being caught, he meets my gaze with confidence.

I spin around to show him the back of my dress and I hear him stifle a laugh behind me.

"Like a rabbit in a snare," he says as I feel him begin to work the knot loose.

"In this rabbit's defense I was expecting help to remove it," I say before I can bite the words back.

I'm standing in the living room of the hottest man I've ever met and I'm putting the thought of another man undressing me into his head. The tugging stops and I feel the warmth of his breath on my bare shoulders. I want to take the words back, but I can't.

"Over my dead body," he says in a low tone.

I glance over my shoulder trying to catch a glimpse of his face.

"Why were you at the church?" I ask as his hands return to my corset.

It's a question I should've asked before getting into his truck. He wasn't on the guest list for the wedding and there wasn't a service planned for that day either. Even if he was just another parishioner seeking spiritual guidance the preacher wasn't due to arrive until closer to the ceremony.

"I was there to get you." His words hit me hard and I find myself spinning to face him just as the corset loosens enough to slip down.

Grabbing the front quick, I stop it from revealing everything to his gaze. But his eyes didn't dip down to catch a peek. They're locked on mine. The heat. The intensity. It's enough to have me melting into a puddle at his feet.

"Why?" I ask letting the word hang heavy between us.

The oceanic depths of his eyes pour into mine letting me see a bit of his soul. I see the answer in them before he answers my question.

"I wasn't going to let you marry that man. You were leaving that church with me one way or another," he says, confirming what I already know.

Standing in the living room, I'm holding up the front of my dress in front of a man who planned to kidnap me from my wedding. I should be running out of this cabin as fast as my feet will carry me. But I'm not scared.

I'm on the verge of kissing this man. This wonderful man who was going to sweep me off my feet and keep me from marrying an unfaithful motherfucker.

Just as I'm about to take the leap, Liam steps back from me and returns his attention to the fishing gear.

"Go change, Alisa," he says. "I haven't been to the grocery store yet and we'll need to catch our dinner."

I slip away to the bathroom, grateful to be free of the layers of tulle, but disappointed that Liam isn't peeling them from my naked body in that bedroom I only caught a glimpse of earlier.

Liam was planning to kidnap me, and he looks at me like he wants to peel my panties off with his teeth.

I lift the collar of his shirt to my nose after I put it on, breathing his warm citrus scent deep into my lungs. The sweatpants are just as soft as they looked. The dove grey fabric is loose around my waist but clings to my thighs and it matches the shirt he gave me to wear.

He's giving me space. Space he thinks I need, but despite the whirlwind events of the day I'm certain that I'm finally right where I need to be.

Liam

"You're handling this well," I tell her after she catches another trout.

At this rate she's going to catch our dinner while I sit beside her looking pretty. I had to bait her hook and give her some basic instruction but as we stand on the bank of a stream that cuts through the back of my property she is showing a knack for fishing. I don't know if it's beginner's luck or if she hustled me.

"I've always wanted to go fishing," she replies, completely ignoring my comment.

It's tempting to ignore the uncomfortable truth floating between us and make small talk about rods and lures. Tempting to brush everything away. But we need to address it, and the sooner the better.

"I kidnapped you," I say watching her closely for a reaction.

Her hazel eyes lock on mine, but they don't widen in fear or surprise. She looks calm like we are just a couple of friends who are fishing on a riverbank together.

"I have a different perspective," she tells me as her line whirls to life again.

Our connection breaks as she returns her attention to her fishing pole.

"How?" The word hangs in the air as she reels in another fish.

I'll be damned if it's not bigger than the other two combined.

"I signed up to marry a stranger. I walked in on him banging my mom. Seems like my judgement of late has been a little shaky."

I shake my head. Her ex is a piece of work to be sure. Cheating on a woman like Alisa should be enough to earn him a diagnosis of some sort. I mean the man really had the perfect woman ready to marry him and follow him around the country and he threw that away for a few minutes of pleasure. With her mom no less.

Maybe that's why she's so mellow about my keeping her. Even if she didn't love the man, I know she had to at least love her mom a little. To be betrayed by the man you were going to marry and your mom all at once must crush her heart.

"I kidnapped you," I repeat.

Her eyebrow quirks in annoyance but she needs to learn that I don't let things go. If something bothers one of us, we're going to talk it out. I've watched my friends fall in love and both Eric and William nearly lost their wives because of miscommunication.

"You took what you wanted," Alisa says.

"Which was you!" I shout.

How can she be so calm about this? She should at the very least be trying to talk me into returning her to town. Asking me to fetch her stuff or take her to a nearby hotel so she can begin piecing her life back together.

"I know," she says.

I shake my head. She signed up to be a mail order bride and she was going to marry that guy without really knowing him. Maybe she is that innocent that she believes in the best of people.

To think she might not have enough experience with men to know how she should be treated sends an uncomfortable twisting sensation through my chest. We're getting nowhere with the kidnapping discussion.

If she's unbothered, then maybe it's not technically kidnapping.

I just have a houseguest that I intend to make my wife.

"A good man would take you to dinner," I tell her.

It's her turn to shake her head.

"I thought a good man asked me to marry him. I was wrong. Good men are kidnapping now," she says while throwing an appraising look my way.

"Only when you're about to marry the wrong man," I say as I rub a fist across my chest.

Just having her call me a good man has my feet feeling lighter and my heart pounding. Not to mention the effect her pouty lipped smile is having on my cock. She wouldn't think of me as a good man if she knew how often I've thought about those pink lips wrapped around my cock.

I've been at half mast ever since I saw her picking out flowers.

"Saving all the women from unhappy marriages?" Her question drags my attention away from her lips and my own spiraling thoughts.

"Just you," I mutter as I reel my line in before casting off again.

"You never told me why you saved me."

"Kidnapping isn't saving," I say with a sigh.

One of us needs to keep our feet on the ground.

"Tomato potato," she says with a laugh, clearly amused by my reticence.

The way her eyes follow my movements has me opening my mouth and letting more words pour out than I intended. I want to give her anything she wants, even if it makes me look like a creep for stalking her.

Because that's exactly what I've done. I stalked and then kidnapped her.

"I saw you on Main at the florist and I followed you. I saw you pick out flowers while his eyes were glued to his phone." I feel her eyes on me as I look straight ahead at the crystalline water. "I watched as you selected your wedding cake, and he didn't even try a single sample. He just took pictures with his phone."

A moment passes in silence as we both watch the river flow by our little fishing spot.

"I picked a real winner, huh?" she says with a mournful sigh.

I can't stand the thought of her upset. Not over an asshole like him.

"Don't worry. I'll never be foolish enough to ignore a beautiful woman like you. He didn't deserve you and his loss is my gain. You're mine now" I say finally tearing my focus away from the water to see her eyes already on me.

The brown has shifted to a light green, her bright eyes sparkling up at me just like I've imagined since the first moment I saw her. Her smile is bright and despite all my reservations about how I've let this relationship begin her happiness fills my chest with pride.

"See? Not kidnapping," she says as her smile stretches into a wry grin.

"Fine." My single word acceptance softened by the smile I feel lifting my whiskered cheeks.

Time floats by as we fish in companiable silence until I finally call it. She's caught enough fish for dinner and our lunch tomorrow. My one bite is too small to keep so I show her how to release the little guy without doing more harm.

"What kind of flowers do you like?" Alisa asks, catching me off guard.

My eyes snap to look at her and the light blush coloring her cheeks might as well be fire engine red for all the alarm bells it sets off. I might be obsessive and possessive, but it would seem my pretty little captive is matching my energy at each step.

I don't know a lot about flowers. No sisters and a sparse dating history have left me with only the basic knowledge. Roses may be a classic gift, but I've never cared for the smell or the thorns that come with them.

I don't want to give her a nonanswer though.

"I don't think about flowers much," I tell her and I see the way her smile begins to dip. "But when you were at the florist, I really liked those pink and blue ones. They looked fluffy and soft."

Her smile turns into a frown. I worry that I've named a flower more suited for a funeral than a wedding when her smile returns full force as her eyes shine up at me with delight.

"Hydrangeas!" she exclaims.

"I don't know what they're called. I just thought they looked pretty."

"They'll be perfect for our wedding."

Alisa

The words slipped out without thought. My cheeks are burning as silence stretches between us. My clammy palms are slippery on the fishing rod. I've crossed the line. I just met this man today. He's everything I could ever want, and I'm worried that I've ruined it before it could truly begin. What man would want a woman who jumps from one man to another on the day of her wedding?

"I'm not picky about food," Liam says breaking the silence. "Mrs. Carmichael hasn't made a cake flavor that I don't like yet."

There is a red tint high on his cheekbones as he stares out at the flowing river. If I'm rushing in head first, at least I'm not alone.

"Red velvet with cream cheese frosting," I offer.

"You'll hear no complaints from me," he replies, turning his head to look up at me.

A tumbleweed blows across the expanse of my mind. If I had two thoughts to rub together it would be two more than I have. I can't think when he's looking at me with those deep blue-green eyes. I can't speak.

"Let's head home," he says. "We still need to fillet your catch."

My stomach turns at the thought of cutting into the fish. As easily as it was to touch the fish when it was dangling from my hook, I can't handle the idea of slicing it with a knife. Its eyes staring up at me in frozen horror.

"You're not going to make me do that, are you?" I ask.

"No, I can carve them up for us," he says with the beginnings of a smirk curling the corner of his mouth.

"Good. You need to make yourself useful," I say.

I expect my words to wipe the smirk from his face at the reminder that I caught the most fish, but I'm surprised to see a grin break out as he laughs at my jab.

"Right? I got hustled by little miss 'I don't know how to fish'. Then you go out and bring in a bigger haul than I ever have. You broke my record."

"This really is my first time!" I cry as I follow him up the muddy riverbank.

The blue cooler full of ice and fish swings as he leads the way. In his other hand he's carrying our fishing poles. Once he's on top of the bank he sets the cooler down on the grass and reaches out a hand, helping me up as my feet slide in the slick dirt underfoot.

"I know. You couldn't even bait your own hook," he says with a chuckle as I find my footing. "Here hold these."

He hands me the fishing rods before picking the cooler back up and then taking my free hand with his. He laces our fingers together as we walk back to his cabin. My heart feels like it's going to beat its way through my rib cage with every step but at the same time I've never felt more comfortable and relaxed with anyone else.

This is everything I wanted. Forget the puffy white dress and the perfect flower arrangements. I would marry this man on a muddy riverbank any day of the week. To an outsider, I'm sure we appear ridiculous. More than enough comments were made about my mental state when I told my coworkers I was leaving my job and becoming a mail order bride.

But that's just it. They're on the outside looking in, they don't get to see what I see. It pains me to admit that they were right about Tyler. None of my friends liked him. They tried to be supportive, but they weren't entirely successful in hiding their true feelings. Everyone but Jenna was skeptical of the mail order bride program I joined. Unlike my coworkers they didn't mock me or call me crazy or insane. They did in-depth research on the company and on Tyler once I told them who I had matched with.

There's a small part of me that's worried they won't like Liam. It's an uncomfortable feeling in my stomach that climbs up my throat like acid reflux. I didn't mind that they didn't like Tyler. Another red flag I shouldn't have ignored. I wasn't invested in our relationship. I wanted my dream wedding, and I wanted a marriage.

Stealing shy glances at Liam from the corner of my eye I can finally admit to myself that I'm grateful for what happened earlier today. If Tyler and I had talked, I might have second guessed my decision to cancel the wedding. He might have talked me into continuing with the ceremony. He might have reminded me of how far our friends and family have traveled to be there. Or how much money I've spent getting everything just right. He didn't care about the flowers, the cake or about the ceremony. The only thing he took note of, despite not chipping in for anything, was the price tag.

I'm where I need to be now though.

I hope Jenna likes him. I hope the other girls don't give him such a hard time. They'll be skeptical. How could they not be? I'm leaping into this with everything I have, and I know I'm not alone. Liam is right there with me.

But their support and their blessing would mean the world to me. My mother and I have never been close, and those few women are the closest I will ever have to sisters.

Liam's hand squeezes mine gently, the calloused palm scratching lightly across my skin. When I look up, I see his warm gaze fixated on me. That look is everything. I see my future. I see my home. I see my family.

If my friends don't like him, it won't stop me from marrying this man. In time they'll get to know him and once they do, I'm sure their opinions will change. But I won't wait for them to get on board.

Every time I look into his eyes I see a piece of his soul. I see the man who fell for me at first sight. The man who couldn't stand the thought of losing me to another. He's honest, brutally so. He was more worried about his kidnapping plans than I was. I couldn't be bothered.

I wanted a man who would be obsessed with me. Who would love me with everything he has. I just had to be engaged to the wrong man to find him.

We haven't said the words yet, but I see them in his eyes every time he looks at me. I'm sure he sees the same when I look at him. One day together and I'm already dreaming of forever.

Tomorrow we'll deal with collecting my belongings, meeting my friends, and dealing with my mother and Tyler. But tonight, I'm going to have dinner with the most gorgeous man I've ever laid eyes on. And then I'm going to climb into his bed and not let him leave until I've given him a dozen reasons to put a ring on my finger.

Liam

I prepare the fish outside. A cheap cutting board on the tailgate of my truck is my usual setup because it's easier to clean. Alisa can't stomach the sight of me fileting the fish, so she heads inside.

With the sun going down the temperature is dropping. By the third fish my hands are chilled, and I regret not wearing gloves.

"I think you need these," Alisa says stepping up beside me with her hand outstretched holding a pair of cut resistant gloves.

Her eyes are firmly on the ground, and I stifle a chuckle. She came out to check on me. She brought me gloves that she thought I would need. She might not be the tough kind of woman that can handle the wilderness. But she doesn't need to know how to clean fish or how to skin a deer. She has me.

"Thank you," I tell her. "I didn't realize how cold my hands would get."

"It didn't feel this cold when we were fishing," she says.

"The temperature drops with the sun. The higher elevation means our warm months and days are shorter," I tell her.

"I saw some potatoes in your kitchen," she replies lingering as I put the gloves on. "I could boil them and make mashed potatoes if you like. I know fish doesn't take that long to cook."

"That'd be perfect," I tell her. "Although you really don't have to cook."

"I want to help. I don't want to be a burden," she says with the slightest downturn of her smile.

"You could never be a burden," I tell her. "Just being here with me is more than enough. Besides, you caught most of our dinner or did you forget?"

She laughs.

"Yeah, I guess I did," she says still giggling.

"I'm almost done," I tell her. "You get started on those potatoes and I'll be inside in just a little bit."

"Don't keep me waiting," she says her eyes darting to mine briefly.

Those eyes sparkle in the orange glow of the sunset. Her hand strikes out swatting my ass as she turns to go, my laughter ringing out behind her.

If I had any doubts that this woman was meant to be mine, they're quashed.

With the gloves on I make quick work of the rest of the fish. Once I'm done it takes two trips to bring everything inside. The filets go on the counter beside the stove Alisa reaching out and turning the oven on to preheat as I go back outside. She already has potatoes boiling on the stove. Her focus is on steaming the asparagus she found in the fridge as I continue to clean up.

The gloves go into the laundry basket, the fish guts and heads go into the trash outside, and the cooler is emptied and set outside to dry. I wash my hands off with the watering hose and spray off my tailgate for good measure. The water coming out of the hose is freezing and by the time I'm back inside my fingers are numb.

The oven beeps and before I can get to the fish Alisa beats me there. She waves me off fetching down the pan from the cupboard. She drizzles it and the fish with olive oil and once she has the filets arranged, she squirts lemon juice on them for good measure.

By the time I've washed my hands she has everything done and I can't fight the urge to smile anymore.

"Who is the burden?" I ask. "Looks to me like you caught dinner and now you're cooking it while all I had to do was cut up some fish."

"Well, you did save me," she replies.

I open my mouth to remind her that I kidnapped her but watching her move around the kitchen I close my mouth and let it go. If she wants to believe that I saved her then I'm never going to be able to convince her otherwise. She is stubborn and hardheaded. She might be squeamish. She might not be able to bait her own hook. But this woman knows what she wants and she's not afraid to ask for it.

Hell, if I didn't stop at the church earlier today, I think Alisa still would have found her way to me. There's something pulling us together, something more than attraction, something bigger than myself. I've heard the other married men around town talking about fate. Is it really a coincidence that of all the men signed up for Pearl's Matchmaking that Alisa chose Tyler? Or was it fate bringing her one step closer to me? Placing her within my reach and giving me the chance to fight for her love?

A month ago, I would have said no. But with Alisa claiming my kitchen as her own, making herself at home as she cooks our dinner, I can't deny fate's hand in bringing us together. I don't know what I did in this life or any other to deserve the woman dancing around my linoleum floor in my T-shirt.

"I'm never going to let you go," I tell her.

She pauses briefly, her smile growing wilder. Her teeth shine under the glow of the kitchen light lending her an almost feral look.

"Well, I hope not," she replies. "Spousal abandonment is a serious crime."

The grin cracking my hard exterior feels strange on my face. I'm head over heels for this woman and by some crazy twist of fate she's right there with me.

"Tomorrow we're gonna get your stuff," I tell her. "If anyone gives you a hard time I'll handle it."

"Looks like I have a big strong man to take care of me," she says her voice dropping to a low husky tone.

Her finger trails down my chest the nail catching lightly on the fabric of my flannel. I stop her progress, capturing her hand with my own and pressing her palm tightly against my chest.

"You have me. For better or worse. For richer or poorer. In sickness and in health. You have me. Always Alisa. My word is my vow. If you marry me, I will move mountains for you. I will crawl across sharp rocks, and I will climb to the tallest peaks for your love."

I don't have a ring but that doesn't stop me. I step back and I drop to one knee. With her hazel eyes on me wide and filled with tears I make it official.

"Alisa, will you marry me?" I ask.

"Yes!" she shouts. "Of course I will."

Standing in the center of our kitchen, with the aroma of our first dinner together cooking, I take my future wife in my arms for the first time. Our noses bump together as our lips meet. Her lips are soft and pliant against my own. The gentle press at odds with the fevered grip her hands have on my shirt. Her nails bite through the fabric as she clutches me close.

I love that she's taller than me, that I don't have to bend or stoop to press my lips to hers. She fits into my arms perfectly and only the oven's timer beeping keeps us from carrying our celebration into the bedroom. Or on the kitchen counter. Or the table.

Alisa pulls away to fetch the food, her cheeks pink and her lips plump from our kisses. I'd rather taste her than our dinner right now, but I don't want her efforts to go to waste.

Sex can wait. I tell myself as I urge my erection to simmer down. We have the rest of our lives to make love, and Alisa deserves more than a rushed coupling on a kitchen counter. When the buttered trout hits my tongue, I nearly moan. It's leagues better than anything I've cooked in this kitchen, and I tell her so.

If I hadn't already proposed I would drop to my knees right here and now.

Alisa

"You don't need to sleep on the couch," I tell him after dinner.

I'm loving that he's enough of a gentleman to offer me his bed. Too bad I'm far more interested in getting him in bed than taking it over.

"I don't think I'll be able to behave myself if we sleep together."

"Good." I step into his space and stroke a hand down his red flannel covered chest. "I don't want you to behave."

"You were going to wait until your wedding to sleep with *him*." He places heavy emphasis on the word like saying my ex's name is taboo.

We talked throughout our dinner without any awkward silences. His friendship with William and Eric came up, and the stories of how both found love through Pearl's.

And we talked about my past relationships and why I waited so long to settle down. Including why I didn't sleep with Tyler. In truth there was never the burning spark of attraction. Nothing like how my body feels ready to burst into flames every time Liam throws so much as a glance my way.

"There wasn't any temptation with *him*," I say echoing his avoidance of the name. "Which in hindsight was a major red flag. It's not like I'm a virgin. There's no point in waiting."

My words hang in the air between us. Liam's eyes follow the contours of my body and for a moment, desire turning his gaze stormy, I'm sure that he's going to give in to my seduction.

"I think I'm worth the wait. You'll just have to suffer until you make an honest man out of me," he says with a playful smirk.

The man has me backed into a corner. He is worth it, and I can't protest unless I want to imply otherwise. Crafty.

I lie down in his king-sized bed alone later that night. For a single man he has an abundance of pillows and a fluffy comforter. When I asked him about it, he turned sheepish before admitting that he bought it all because he wanted to feel like he was sleeping on a cloud. I hate that it's white. No pattern or embroidery to be seen. The sheets, pillowcases, and the comforter are all bright white.

But it does feel like sleeping on a cloud. Maybe I can get him to order it in grey so that we can sleep on a rain cloud.

Stretching my arms out I can't touch the sides of the bed. My hands slide through the cool crisp sheets, and I admit to myself that sleeping alone in this bed isn't the worst thing.

The night before my big church wedding I couldn't sleep a wink. Tonight, I fall asleep within moments, comforted by the thought of Liam lying on the couch just outside the bedroom door.

Liam

She texts the group once I'm awake. Her phone buzzing with the confirmation texts as we sit down in the kitchen.

"Did you tell them about us?" I ask as I pour us both a cup of coffee.

It might be breakfast with the girls, but I won't be able to make it to the diner without caffeine in my veins.

"Nope." she replies. "I want to explain everything at once. And I don't want them judging you before they meet you."

"I'm not worried," I tell her thinking about her ex.

The man fucked her mom. If her friends didn't like the guy before everything came to light, they must have pretty good bullshit detectors. I have nothing to hide from them.

Alisa is a ball of energy next to me as we drive down the mountain. Her leg is bouncing up and down betraying her nerves. With her life changing so much over the last twenty-four hours I'm not surprised she's anxious.

Considering how small Crescent Ridge is I'm sure we're going to run into her ex or her mother. Possibly both. I'm sure neither will linger in town once word begins to spread about yesterday morning. This small town protects its own. Alisa had already captured the local hearts before I made my move. They'll have her back.

"Alisa!" a tall brunette shouts while waving at us from the sidewalk as I park in front of *Lenny's*.

"Jenna!" Alisa returns in an excited wave.

"Tell me everything!" Jenna says wrapping Alisa in a hug as soon as she steps out of the truck.

"Inside," Alisa says pressing a guiding hand to her friend's back before glancing over her shoulder to make sure I'm following them into the restaurant.

Jenna's blue eyes swing to mine and I see the moment she clocks our relationship. I haven't given Alisa a ring yet and we're not cuddled up, but she can read the chemistry between us.

"Now *that* is what I call an upgrade," Jenna stage whispers to Alisa as I follow behind them.

"Stop ogling my man," Alisa says swatting at her friend just as we arrive at a corner booth.

Three more women sit around the table, each one glancing from Alisa to me as they all voice their concern for her.

"Obviously I'm not marrying Tyler," Alisa says once we're seated. "This is Liam, my white knight."

Introductions go around the table as I try to remember all the details I'm given. Kat is short for Katherine. She and her sister Camille grew up next door to Alisa and she's their unofficial third sister despite the pair being platinum blondes who barely break the five-foot mark in height. Victoria is a redhead with more freckles than a dalmatian has spots and a thick pair of glasses that make her green eyes appear comically large.

They listen with rapt attention as Alisa describes finding Tyler and her mother in the church.

"On the day of your wedding!" Jenna shouts.

"And she thought you would still marry him after finding them like *that*?" Victoria asks her tone colored with her anger.

"All true," Alisa murmurs as Kat and Camille add their outrage to the mix.

"And?" Jenna leads a moment later. "Where did blondie come into the mix?"

I ignore the jab. It's barely a poke really. Doesn't stop Alisa from standing up for me though.

"His name is Liam," she says shooting a pointed look at her friend, her meaning clear. "And we're getting married."

The table goes silent at her revelation. Each of the women processing her announcement. Wendy, the waitress who has worked at *Lenny's* my entire life heard Alisa too and she comes bustling over before the women can voice their opinions.

"Liam!" she shouts smacking my shoulder with a laminated menu that's older than me. "Where is my invitation young man?"

"You're invited," I tell her ignoring the sting from her attack. "We just haven't worked out the details yet."

"I used up all my PTO for this," Kat says with a wince.

"I have that business trip coming up and I can't cancel it," Victoria adds.

"We'll pick a day that works for everyone," I reassure them. "Family is everything and we want you all to be there when we get hitched."

Kat, Camille, and Victoria all seem mollified and I'm counting this introduction as a success when I look over to see Alisa and Jenna locking eyes. I watch eyebrows dance and lips purse as they carry on a silent conversation.

"Today?" Jenna asks after a moment.

My eyebrows raise and I see the other women widen their eyes in shock. I figured we could have a courthouse wedding today or tomorrow, but Alisa would want a bigger ceremony for her family.

"We are all together," Victoria offers in a meek voice. "And we have the dresses, flowers, and cake."

"We wanted to see if you wanted to smash the wedding cake or eat it," Kat says with a smile.

"My room at the inn looks like a flower festival," Camille adds. "We didn't want the arrangements to go to waste."

I do my best to hide my shock. I expected I would need to win them over, even have a few people like Wendy or Poppy vouch for me. But despite the sudden turn of events all of Alisa's friends seem to be on board.

"Today," Alisa says, turning to me with a smile. "Do you think your friends can make it?"

My grin is probably answer enough but still I say the words.

"I'll make some calls," I tell her. "Have breakfast with your friends and I'll get the rest ready for this afternoon."

Twenty separate phone calls later and I have things in motion. Eric and William are on their way into town with their wives in tow. Preacher John is available to officiate so long as we can get down to the courthouse before they break for lunch to get our marriage license. And all the locals I can reach are closing shops early to be at the wedding.

"Mrs. Carmichael will have our cake ready in time," I tell Alisa as I walk over to the booth. "Red velvet with cream cheese frosting, right?"

"Right," she replies beaming at me.

"And I got Mrs. Clarke to sell me all her hydrangeas," I tell her joining the women at the table.

"Jenna's going to take me dress shopping after breakfast," she replies with a twinkle in her eye. "I don't want to use anything from yesterday especially not that corset contraption."

Wendy brings me a plate of pancakes the minute my butt hits the chair. The women have already eaten but they are in no rush to leave as they begin to bombard me with questions. Clearly the shock has lifted, and the interrogation has begun.

"Where do you live?" Kat asks.

"Do you have any single firefighter friends?" Camille follows.

"Have you been married before?" Jenna asks directly.

"Mountain cabin, not too far from town. Yes, and they will all be at the church this afternoon. No," I answer back rapidly between bites.

"He'll do," Jenna says with a reluctant smile.

Four hours later we have the license, the cake, and the flowers. I'm left waiting at an altar next to Preacher John as Eric and William stand next to me as groomsmen. We're all dressed in flannel and jeans. There aren't any formal boutiques in Crescent Ridge and Alisa wanted us to look like the mountain men we are, so flannel it was.

I watch as Kat, Camille, Victoria, and finally Jenna all walk up the aisle in matching blue bridesmaid dresses. The satin formal wear at odds with the causal dress on my side of the altar.

Everything in front of me fades away when Alisa enters the church. Gone is the fancy dress from yesterday and in its place is a delicate white sundress that shows off her long legs. Thankfully, everyone is watching the bride walk down the aisle so only she sees me adjust my jeans to hide my erection. Her shy smile turns into a grin as we lock eyes as she walks down the aisle to me.

The second I take her hands in mine the rest of the ceremony is a blur. I repeat my vows after the preacher and wait as Alisa does the same. Suddenly we've reached the best part of the ceremony.

"You may kiss the bride," Preacher John says a moment before Alisa, and I melt into one another.

I can hear her friends cheer, but I can't be bothered by their presence or propriety as I hold Alisa close. Her dress is simple, and it molds around her curves, offering no resistance to my embrace like the stiff tulle and satin wedding dress she wore yesterday. Cheers turn to giggles as we break apart. I think I hear Shawn from the station whistle, but I don't turn my head to check.

The entire town is crammed into the church. I even saw Lily and Daniel with their four children earlier. Everyone showed up to watch us get married and I think the only two souls not present are Alisa's mother and ex.

Alisa

Our ceremony was surprisingly well put together considering it was arranged this very morning. I'm sure it's because of how the town came together to support us. Everyone I've met over the last week is there. We even had a photographer step forward to get pictures of the wedding party after the ceremony.

"Is it just me or does every man on this mountain look like they've stepped out of a calendar?" Jenna asks between poses.

"So many men in uniform," Victoria murmurs as she pushes up her glasses.

I follow her gaze to a man who is mingling with several of Liam's firefighter buddies. Like the sheriff he's still in his park ranger uniform. His dark hair curls over his ears at odds with his starched green polo tucked into his khaki pants. I can see why my shy librarian friend is staring.

"I can ask Liam if he's single," I offer as the photographer directs us into another pose.

"No!" Victoria whisper yells drawing attention from the ranger and several other people nearby.

I know at least one photo is going to have my bridesmaid blushing from the roots of her hair to her toes.

"You made him look!" she scolds.

"How dare we get the hot ranger to notice you," Kat teases.

"What a shame that he's looking at you like he wants to tie you to his bed and never let you leave," Camille adds.

We watch as Liam and his friends pose for photos before we're all brought together. Liam's hands are hot on my hips, and I would rather be alone in our cabin than here with our friends. The man has been proper all day and it's killing me. But this is our wedding, and I won't ruin this for my husband. Even though he looks delectable with his beard groomed and his flannel shirt paired with well-worn jeans.

He's the man I always longed for when I was lonely. A man larger than life who focuses his attention entirely on me. Our wedding is nothing like the one I planned for yesterday and it's perfect. I feel more like a bride in my cotton sundress than I did standing in his living room in that satin ballgown.

The reception is held at a dance hall where we cut the cake, dance, and celebrate until the sky turns dark. Liam's eyes darken every time they find me. We spend most of the party side by side but anytime I step away to talk to someone or go to the bathroom his eyes follow me. A warm flush heats my neck and cheeks as his eyes track my movement.

When we share our first dance, I make sure I stay close letting my curves brush against his body with every movement. The heat building in his eyes turns them a darker blue as we sway together. His fresh citrus scent washes over me as I rest my head on his chest, the flannel soft under my cheek.

"Ready to go home?" Liam asks once our dance is over.

"We can't be rude!" I scold him despite the temptation to run out of the reception like my dress is on fire.

"Daniel had a courthouse wedding. Same with William. Eric had an actual wedding, but they barely made it to the reception before they ducked out. Trust me, we have done our due diligence."

That's all I need to hear.

"Let's go," I say tugging him by the hand to lead him off the dance floor.

Back at the cabin when it is just me and Liam alone once again, I feel myself trembling with excitement. Everything that had felt inevitably bland with Tyler is the opposite for us. Just Liam holding my hand is enough to send shivers down my spine and heat building low in my belly.

"I don't want to rush this." He said as we stepped through the front door of his cabin once again. Our cabin.

At odds with his good intentions, the second the door bangs closed behind us his lips are on mine. Warm and wet they slip and slide as my hands rip open the front of his flannel, buttons pinging on the hardwood floor as they fall.

"Promised I would take this slow," he growls into my ear when I reach for the belt buckle on his jeans.

He doesn't stop me from unbuttoning his jeans or from shoving his boxers down to expose his cock.

"Slow is overrated," I damn near purr as I take him in hand.

He's thick at the base with a long tapered length that ends with a mushroom shaped tip. The dark veins running the length stand out as he flexes in my hand.

"Agreed," he groans as I drag my hand along his cock, my nails lightly scraping the underside as I go.

"Such a pretty cock," I compliment as he thrusts into my hands. "I can't wait to taste it."

"Later," he growls.

Pulling away from my touch he steps out of his clothes leaving them puddled on the living room floor. Taking my hand eagerly in his, Liam leads me to the bedroom.

I kick off my sandals in a rush as I dart after him. He stops just before the bedroom door dragging a hand down his face as he mutters to himself.

"What's wrong?" I ask.

He doesn't immediately answer my question. His dark blue-green eyes find mine and I see the twinkle of mischief shining there just before he lunges. A second later he's holding me close to his chest as he carries me through our bedroom door.

"Almost missed a tradition," he says before setting me down on the bed.

I begin to protest when he sinks down to his knees at the end of the bed. He flips up the hem of my dress to expose my white lace undies. The puff of cold air hitting the damp fabric raises goosebumps on my arms. Feeling his eyes lingering on my center I try to calm my racing heart with steady breaths as he reaches out to move the scrap of fabric aside. The rough pad of his finger brushes across my clit as he bares my core to his heated gaze.

"Look how pretty you are dripping for me," he says as he presses a finger into my slickness.

My inner muscles cling to the digit as he withdraws, unwilling to release him from my grasp entirely. With a chuckle he pushes back in and he finds a rhythm that makes my breathing come out in short halting puffs. A second later his tongue finds my clit, the rough texture stroking across my sensitive flesh has me arching my back as my hands scramble to grip the sheets.

Soft circles of his tongue drive me wild as he adds a second finger to my core. My orgasm doesn't build slowly. One moment he's teasing his tongue around my clit without touching it and the next he sucks it into his mouth causing me to fall apart with a shocked scream.

Boneless with satisfaction I'm little more than a limp noodle as Liam peels my underwear off completely. I help him with my sundress when he looks for a zipper that doesn't exist. The thin cotton peels away easily leaving me entirely bare beneath his gaze.

"Lovely. Absolutely lovely," he growls, eyes locked on mine.

He takes his time entering me, slowly pushing in inch by inch until we're fully connected. The pleasant stretch of his cock filling me eases a tension I wasn't aware of until now.

"I love you, Liam," I whisper into the heavy air between us.

"Love. You. More," he whispers back punctuating each word with a gentle thrust of his hips.

We move together, our bodies meeting slowly at first and then faster as sweat begins to bead on Liam's brow. The low heat building in my core is flaring into molten lava with each press of his hips. Our breaths are mingling in the cold room as I touch every inch of his body I can reach.

My nails sink into the skin of his shoulders and that's when his control snaps. He pounds his cock into me like he's trying to hammer a nail into a stubborn piece of wood. His pelvis slams into my clit as I fall apart screaming his name.

Two thrusts later and Liam is straining above me as his seed coats my inner walls in a warm spray.

"Definitely love you more," he mumbles later when we're sprawled out in a messy heap under the covers.

I go to argue but yawn instead.

Let him win this one. I think to myself. I have the beginning of forever in my arms and all the time in the world to debate with my husband.

Liam

The day after we're married, I don't want to leave the cabin, but I need to report for my shift at the station. As a volunteer I don't need to work as many days as Shawn and the others, but I do need to work a few shifts every month. Skills need to be utilized every so often or they become rusty.

We get the call for a structure fire in the afternoon, and we're dispatched to an old cabin close to the river. No one has lived there in decades but if the fire were left unattended it could begin burning the trees around it and be the start of a wildfire.

Then there is the question of how the building was set on fire to begin with.

Captain Thomas shares a worried look with our crew once we have the fire contained. The hoses are packed up and we're all changing out of our gear when he calls us over. I store my gear with the others on the firetruck despite my own pickup being parked behind the bright red engine. It comes in handy to have a second vehicle on site in case we find someone injured.

"I've called Sheriff Larson," he says as we assemble. "Looks like we have a firebug. Find anything unusual?"

"He left gasoline cans," Corey says pointing towards the tree line.

"Looks like a rush job," Shawn says scratching his chin. "This far out they had all the time in the world to make it burn evenly but they lit the fire and ran."

It could be a couple of teens trying to rebel. It could be a small fire that grew out of control and the vandals fled in fear. No one wants an arson charge. But my gut is twisting itself in knots.

"I need to check on Alisa," I tell the group.

I expect jabs and jeers about my newlywed status but all I receive are solemn nods. It only adds to my worry as they all reach the same conclusion. Everyone knows I'm a volunteer firefighter and it wouldn't take much to find out when I'm scheduled to work. This fire was lazy with no clear purpose.

A distraction.

"Call the sheriff and send him to my cabin," I tell Shawn as I run for my truck.

People bicker in Crescent Ridge. But there are only two people who could be angry enough to cause property damage and harm. Alisa's mother went home before our wedding. She sent my wife an apology text this morning that somehow didn't take any accountability or express any remorse for her actions. While I'm sure that my wife is never going to make true peace with her mother in this lifetime, my gut tells me the older woman really is gone from Crescent Ridge.

But Tyler is still in town.

Alisa

"You embarrassed me!" Tyler screams as he waves a gun at me.

When I heard the car drive up to the cabin, I thought it was Liam coming home early or maybe Lily or Jenna dropping by for a chat. I never thought when I threw open the front door that he would be on the other side.

I started to yell at him when I noticed the black handgun he was pointing at me. Without a word he forced me back into the cabin leaving the door open behind him. The stench of stale beer lingers in the air as I watch him stumble around with heavy footsteps and I know without a doubt he's drunk.

"Things worked out for the best," I try to say despite trembling lips as I hope that Tyler is too drunk to aim his gun accurately. "I mean you didn't want to marry me."

"No, I didn't," Tyler snarks. "You looked hotter in your picture. Less like a stuck-up prude."

My pride bristles but I don't argue with him. I need to get away from this psycho but until I have an opportunity to escape, I need to keep him calm. My breathing has become shallow, and I force myself to take a deep fortifying breath. The stale scent of beer is still there but I focus on the sweet pine scent that wafts through the open door. The faint trace of citrus that clings lightly to the entire house.

"We're not right for each other," I try again.

He rolls his eyes as he begins to pace the length of the living room.

"Obviously," he grumbles more to himself than me.

I edge towards the kitchen, debating if I can get out the back door before he can fire a shot.

"But you didn't have to marry someone else the day after you left me at the altar!" he yells swinging the gun back to me.

I freeze in place raising my hands up in front of me in a soothing gesture.

"I fell in love," I tell him.

"More like lust," he mumbles. "I would have treated you better if you had spread your legs that fast for me."

"You mean like fucking my mom?" I snarl, all thoughts of keeping him calm deserting me as my anger flares.

My eyes dart to the door when a shadow forms on the hardwood floor. With Tyler's attention focused on me I try to keep the relief from showing on my face. Tyler is drunk but that doesn't mean he's dumb. And with that pistol he is far from harmless.

"She came on to me," he protests. "Practically begged for my cock."

I don't care who started the affair, as far as I'm concerned it was a betrayal by both and led me to the man I love. But Liam needs a distraction and Tyler is so focused on yelling at me that he doesn't hear the floorboards by the front door creak.

"You fell for her lies," I say to goad him. "No one wants to marry you."

"You bitch!" he shouts a moment before Liam tackles him from behind.

The gun slides out of his hand as Liam pins him to the floor with ease. I run forward and pick it up before Tyler can make a grab for it.

"Sheriff is on his way," Liam tells me.

"How did you know he was here?" I ask Liam as he holds Tyler down while we wait for the sheriff to arrive.

"He started a fire," Liam says smacking Tyler's head onto the floor. "No one on the ridge is stupid enough to start a fire this close to the dry season. It was obviously a distraction."

"Can't prove I did it," Tyler slurs.

"Attempted murder," I tell him ticking off charges with my fingers. "Trespassing. Arson."

Liam chuckles darkly just as red and blue flashing lights illuminate the room through the windows.

"Shame he got here so fast," he says in a low tone with his lips next to Tyler's ear. "Saved you from a well-deserved ass kicking."

Epilogue

Liam

Six Months Later

It's a rare day when I wake up in bed alone. Normally Alisa is sound asleep when I start my day in the workshop, but when I wake up today the grey sheets beside me are cold and crisp.

My wife got up early.

The sun is just beginning to rise with orange and yellow rays shining through the gossamer curtains of our bedroom. I never get up before the sun, but curiosity and the scent of fresh coffee lures me from the warm bed.

I make my way towards the kitchen wiping sleep from my eyes as I search for my wife.

"Morning," I greet Alisa when I find her by the stove.

She's dressed in nothing more than an old T-shirt of mine as she flips the bacon sizzling in the pan.

"Good morning, my dear husband," she replies sweetly.

I walk up behind her pressing a soft kiss to her cheek as I hug her close.

"Too early," I mumble into her shoulder as I cling to her while she works.

"Better get used to it," she says as she continues to make our breakfast.

"Why?" I ask.

She waits to answer my question until she has all the bacon cooling on a plate and the stove burners turned off. Spinning to face me with a coy smile her hazel eyes sparkle with joy as she wraps her arms around me.

A suspicion forms in my mind as I take notice of the kitchen. The kitchen table is covered in a white linen table-cloth with freshly picked flowers sitting in a vase at the center. She's cooked eggs, sausage, bacon and toast. My heart thumps heavily in my chest before I remind myself that we're only halfway to our first anniversary. I didn't forget a special day, but she's celebrating something all right.

"To my understanding babies rarely sleep through the night," she says with a pointed look.

It takes a moment for her words to penetrate my brain still foggy from sleep. But when they do a broad grin spreads across my face.

"We're pregnant?" I ask in a soft tone.

We've been trying for the last few months, but I didn't expect it would happen so fast. My heart beats fast, damn near threatening to burst from my chest as Alisa's eyes fill with tears and she gives me a shaky nod.

"We're pregnant," I say unable to keep the excitement from my voice.

I cup Alisa's face in my hands as I press soft kisses across her forehead, down her nose, and finally her plump lips. Our sweet kiss turns feral fast. Tongues tangle as my hands thread their way into her hair, the strands wrapping around my knuckles as I deepen our kiss.

"Sit down," she says when we break apart.

The gentle press of her palms on my shoulders has my ass hitting the chair a moment later. The walnut backing is chilly against spine as Alisa sinks to her knees on the hardwood.

"Relax," she purrs running a palm down my chest.

When she gets to the stretchy waistband of my pajama pants her fingers slip under and pull them down before I can protest.

"Alisa-" I begin to say but she shushes me.

"Don't try to stop me," she says in a pout. "I've been wanting to do this for ages, but I didn't want to waste a drop while we were trying to get pregnant."

I fight back a moan when her lips wrap around the head of my cock. Her wet mouth swallows the length with ease.

I bump the back of her throat, and she swallows around me, her mouth convulsing. I lean back in my chair as she begins to drag her mouth up and down my cock. Her lips form a tight seal around me, the suction firm as her mouth milks me. Each pass of her mouth drives me higher until I feel the tingling sensation at the base of my spine.

I tap her shoulder, but she ignores my warning, and I come spilling my seed down her throat. She swallows every drop.

"You are the sweetest woman. I don't know what I ever did to deserve you," I say with a warm smile as she grins up at me.

She slides onto my lap and feeds me bites of the breakfast she made. She chatters about how Lily is pregnant again and our babies will be born around the same time. I take the bites of bacon with a wide grin on my face as she talks about milestones and babyproofing the cabin.

Her bare thighs are visible where her shirt has ridden up on her lap and I feel my cock rising to half past as my hands stroke the smooth skin.

"Maybe we should start practicing for making this baby a little brother or sister," I whisper into her ear delighting in the way she shivers in my arms.

Her ass presses against my hard cock when she shifts on my lap. My wife isn't even trying to be subtle about grinding her pussy on me.

"Yeah?" she asks with a coy smile.

We laugh as she gets off my lap in a hurry and runs towards the bedroom with me hot on her heels. Six months in and we can't keep our hands off each other. Not a day goes by that we're not making love in our bed or fucking on the kitchen counter.

My wife is gorgeous, brilliant, and pregnant with our first child. We have a cabin close enough to our friends in town but far enough away that we have our own piece of quiet.

I don't know how I got so lucky to have Alisa love me, but I'll never stop being grateful that a woman as amazing as her could fall in love with someone like me.

Fate brought her to the mountain, but our love is what will keep us here. Love for each other and our small family. Love for the town that claimed her as one of their own. And love for the mountain that we all call home.

The End

Ready to meet Corey's bride? Willow inherited her father's gambling debt and now owes the Italian Mafia. Can she escape the danger chasing her in Mountain Man's Sweet Mail Order Bride?

***

Sign up for my newsletter or follow me on Amazon or Facebook to stay updated on new releases.

Mountain Man's Sweet Mail Order Bride

Jacqueline Carmine

Willow

"Bring the money on Monday or you'll work off the debt another way," the man standing above me grunts.

He leaves me laying on the linoleum flooring of my kitchen as he shows himself out of my small apartment. I'm still wearing the uniform from my job at L&P where I work all day operating a robot to spot weld aluminum pieces into a completed brake bracket. The navy pants are worn thin at the knees and pockets and permanently stained with grease. The matching long sleeved shirt is no better. My short blonde hair sticks to my forehead with sweat from the bump cap I wear for the endurance of my twelve-hour shift.

When I came home, I didn't notice the broken lock on the door. Too tired from my shift I ignored all the warning signs. I always lock the door when I leave. It should have occurred to me that I didn't have to use my key to get inside. As soon as I stepped into the kitchen his fist shot out striking me across my face and I went down like a sack of rocks.

Still dazed I was helpless to resist when he wrapped his hand around my throat as he sat on my chest. Dark spots were clouding my vision by the time he let me breathe. This threat isn't idle and while I didn't recognize him, I know who he works for.

When my father died three months ago, I didn't know that he had a gambling problem. He hid it well and it was a shock to find out that he owed the Carrisi's almost two hundred thousand dollars. If he owed a bank that money his debt would die with him. But he borrowed money from the mafia, and they want that money back in full plus interest. His debt is now mine.

I make good money at the factory. I have seniority and paid time off and after five years of working for the company I'm maxed out on the pay scale. I was saving to buy a house, but my father's debt cleaned out my bank account and my savings.

Unfortunately, even if I was promoted to the top of management tomorrow, I still wouldn't make enough to pay all my bills and to cover the debt my father accrued. Certainly not in the time limit the Carrisi family enforcer gave me. In a different city I could go to the police. Not in

Chicago. The Carrisi's run this city from the top down. A police report would only exacerbate my situation with the addition of dirty cops.

I stumble to the sink turning the tap to cold before I grab a dish rag soaking it in the water. The cold compress against my swollen cheek does little for the burning pain but it's better than nothing.

I've done everything I can think of and it's not enough. I sold my father's house and everything inside it that had any kind of value. With the sale and my savings, I've cut the debt in half. A hundred thousand dollars still owed, and I kick myself every day for not taking the money from the sale and fleeing the country.

My father didn't have a car, another warning sign ignored. He swore up and down that at his age he could take the bus or walk anywhere that he needed to go. Considering how often my mother had to nag him to walk around our neighborhood when she was alive, I should have known better.

No life insurance. No savings.

I slump into a rickety kitchen chair as my mind races, the spindles pressing uncomfortably into my back, and I struggle not to fall into despair. It's been too much these last three months. Sorting my father's estate and grieving his death.

Even at the funeral I knew it would come to this.

There's no way I'll ever be able to pay off that debt in time. I need a way out. Reaching into my purse, I pull out the flyer I grabbed on my way out of the factory. One of the guys on the welding line brought it in to have a laugh.

Pearl's Mail Order Brides the flyer says in bold print at the top. I glance down at the details written below again considering the impossible.

To marry a stranger? Can I do it?

I never had the white picket fence dream all the other little girls did. I didn't play act marriages in kindergarten or read bridal magazines in high school. But I thought when I married it would be to someone whom I loved. Like my parents. Thinking back to the last few years, I see it with a sudden clarity that makes my chest ache.

That's when it all went downhill.

Watching my mother slowly die of cancer is what broke my father. He never truly recovered from her death. He was a shadow of his former self, and I missed the signs that he was forming an addiction to fill the hole she left behind.

I pull up the website on my phone with a heavy heart. This isn't how I saw my future but if I don't find a way out, I'm not going to have one. I know what happens to the women who work for the Carrisi family.

They would have me earn the money on my back, entertaining a variety of men as a prostitute under Carrisi management. Even if I could stomach it, I know that wouldn't be the end. They run Chicago and everyone knows it. If I were to earn the total sum, they would add fees for setting me up with clients. Extra interest added for not paying the debt in full. I would work for them until I died.

I need out.

With less than a week I need an exit strategy. They want the money on Monday. Knowing the way they operate, I need to be gone by the weekend to give myself enough time to make a clean getaway.

Sitting at the table, stomach growling in my grease covered uniform I fill out the forms for the background check and identity verification. Once everything is submitted, I work on preparing my dinner. There's nothing to do about it now. Pushing aside my panic and worries I work on making myself a sausage, egg and cheese burrito, letting my mind focus on the task in front of me rather than the reality crumbling around me.

Corey

It feels a bit silly waiting for my future wife at the airport. For all the success of mail order brides in our small town, all my friends still poked fun at me for signing up. My stomach is twisting with anxiety as people mill about around me and I feel odd standing empty handed. I should've brought flowers or made a welcome sign. Something to make her smile.

I glance down to the itinerary on my phone again. I check the flight information she provided against the computer displays overhead. I'm not late. I got here early just in case her arrival was ahead of schedule. Now her plane is about to begin unloading and I'll finally meet my bride.

She's planned everything down to the hour and made it so that all I need to do is show up on time and say I do during our vows. The itinerary is like a weighted blanket warming my soul and soothing the frayed edges of my mind.

It's all been a whirlwind ever since I got Willow's message on the app. Absolutely stunning with short blonde hair and sage green eyes, I almost didn't believe she messaged me on purpose. Or that she was real. I'm not sure I'll really believe it until I see her in person. She looks like a pixie brought to life. Far too bright and perky to marry a dull man like me.

That she wants to move out here within a week of us matching just makes it all feel more surreal. I should pump the brakes and tell her it's a bad time. But I know that if I do, I'll just keep putting it off and I'll never get to meet the woman behind those soulful eyes. A woman who just might be the perfect match for me. The type of woman used to taking control and making decisions. The exact kind of partner I need. I don't know what she needs from me in return but whatever it is I'll strive to provide it.

Her messages were pointed and direct revealing a woman used to speaking her mind. The one phone call before she bought her plane ticket did nothing to counteract that impression. Her low-pitched voice was soothing and soft even if her words were sharp and bold.

Just the memory of that ordinary conversation is enough to have my cock straining against my zipper. Something that only adds to the flurry of panic swirling around in my head. I became a firefighter to help people.

When we're out on the call there is no time for panic. I need to move and get the job done every second that I waste could be another life lost. In the field I'm decisive and quick.

In my day-to-day life, however, I'm the opposite. My friends know not to leave decisions in my hands. Don't make me choose where to eat. Don't make me choose an activity. My mind will race, and I'll try to weigh every option over and over until eventually I'm sitting on my couch calling off the entire outing.

Willow's proposal took a heavy weight off my chest. Answering her questions and letting her lead our conversations made it easy to talk to her. It makes my hands shake to think of how much I've revealed to a stranger over the last few days. And I know almost nothing about her.

I want to know her. I want to know everything about her. But our conversations were limited, and she had a lot of questions. I want to be irritated but I can't. A single woman moving out to marry a man she's never met sounds like the beginning of a horror movie. I could be anyone. Could be a murderer. Could be some psycho who would lock her up in an underground bunker somewhere in the woods.

I'm not. She doesn't know that.

With how quickly she arranged our marriage and her move out date I can only assume she's running from something. And what's even more insane about this whole ordeal is that I want to protect her. If all I can do is give her security and peace of mind that's a start.

Because the thought of someone or something scaring her enough to have her flee to our small mountain town is enough to have my hackles rising.

I don't know what she's running from but if it follows her to Crescent Ridge there will be hell to pay.

Willow

The airport in Bramble, Colorado is tiny with a single baggage claim and wide glass windows that show off the evergreen mountain peaks a short distance away. I step out with my few fellow passengers into the lobby and my eyes immediately snag on my fiancé.

He cuts an attractive figure in a green plaid flannel shirt and dark wash denim jeans. With dark tousled hair and a soft smile, he looks like the boy next door. The guy you compare every boyfriend to and secretly wish you'd made a move when you had the chance. This close it's clear that he didn't use any kind of filter to make his profile photos look better. This mountain man is just that handsome.

"Willow?" he asks with a wide grin as I approach.

"That's Mrs. Peters to you," I reply with a matching smile.

"Almost," Corey replies.

When I'm close enough, he reaches out and pulls me into a firm hug. My fiancé is a hugger. Never one to be overly affectionate with strangers I don't expect to enjoy it.

But I do.

I melt into the hard planes of Corey's chest, his flannel shirt soft beneath my cheek and his hands warm against my back despite the layers separating us. For the first time since my father's death all my tension fades away leaving me in the arms of a stranger who feels like home. The scent of vanilla and cinnamon hits my nose making me think of childhood holidays spent with my family.

My vision blurs unexpectedly and I blink rapidly to clear it. Spine stiffening, I pull away before I'm ready. I can't seem like a basket case five minutes after meeting the man I'm going to marry.

"I didn't think you were real," Corey says in a soft voice as I slip out of his arms.

"As real as they come," I reply looking past him at the mountain vista visible through the windows.

I feel if I look at him directly, I'll be struck mute or worse my childhood stutter will come roaring back to life. The man is too gorgeous. It's ridiculous that he felt the need to find a bride through a service like Pearl's. This man should have a wife and two kids with a white picket fence. Not a bride running from the Italian Mafia. If I think about it too much the guilt will have me calling off the wedding.

But I need this. I need Corey's last name and the safety of a new home where no one has heard of the Carrisi family.

"Let's get your bags," Corey says placing a hand on my lower back to guide me over to the lone baggage claim.

I never traveled much before my father's death. A few trips to visit distant family once or twice when I was a child. I remember waiting ages to get my suitcase then but now my luggage beat me off the plane. The lone black suitcase looks too small to contain my entire life, but it does.

"Movers bringing the rest?" Corey asks as he grabs my suitcase with one large hand.

"Nope," I say. "This is it."

A faint pink flush sits high on his cheeks and I watch with fascination as it creeps up to his ears. I should be embarrassed not to have more to my name but when it came time to pack, I couldn't justify bringing an assortment of knickknacks that have no sentimental value. I liked each and every bauble, but they were just things. I can buy new trinkets once I settle in and find a job.

And I never planned to hire movers for my furniture. My location could be leaked easily through any company I hired and one day I could answer the door to see a mafia enforcer come to collect.

"Just as well," Corey adds after a moment. "Our house is rather cluttered."

My head jerks up in surprise and he misreads my look.

"Swear I'm not a hoarder," he says sheepishly. "But I do like to collect things."

His dark brown eyes catch on mine and I'm helpless to look away. Mistaking my silence for judgement he quickly begins to ramble.

"There is room for all your things though! I made room in the closet and the dresser, and we can get new furniture and décor of course. None of the curtains match and I heard Liam's wife talking about fruit kitchens. Like if you want a lemon kitchen or apple kitchen or anything really, we can redecorate-"

I slap my palm over his mouth to stop the onslaught of words. His eyes are wide with panic above an aquiline nose, the whites of his eyes overshadowing his dark irises.

"I'm sure your home is lovely," I tell him while waiting for him to settle. "I like collecting things too but when it came down to packing, I thought I needed a fresh start. And trust me your house wouldn't have enough room for it all."

Corey seems mollified by my admission although I hear him mutter something that sounds like *would've found room* behind my hand, but I can't be sure. I pull away acutely aware that I was just plastered against his body for the second time in the last hour before reminding myself that I'm marrying this man. Surely, he's going to expect a lot more physical affection than a mere hug.

A man doesn't get married expecting to take a vow of celibacy. Raking my gaze down his body again I can't ignore the way my body heats under his gaze. I would have to be dead not to find the idea of sex with this man appealing.

"So," Corey says after clearing his throat. "I downloaded your itinerary and if we want to stay on track we need to hit the road."

For a moment I'm struck speechless again. No one ever follows my itineraries. Every friend group treated them like a chore and even my own father couldn't hide his annoyance. But this man, who is barely more than a stranger not only read the schedule but also memorized it?

If I hadn't already proposed, I would hit my knees right here in the airport lobby and beg him to marry me. Corey's smile is crooked as he waits for me to get myself in gear. He's trying to stick to the plan I laid out but he's not rushing me. He's giving me a chance to back out or slow down if I'm not ready.

"Beautiful day for a wedding," I say in response.

I'm ill-prepared for the look of joy that spreads across his face. His warm hand grabs mine while his other carries my suitcase like it's no heavier than a purse.

"I'd marry you any day," he says over his shoulder as he leads me out of the airport.

It's a good thing he's leading otherwise he would see the bright red blush burning my cheeks at his unexpectedly sweet words. If he doesn't stop with the charming words and considerate manner I might just overheat and melt into a puddle of goo at his feet.

Corey

My heart sticks in my throat as we drive up the mountain to Crescent Ridge. I half expected to return bride-less to a quiet home. But Willow arrived just as she said she would. The lack of possessions only confirms my suspicions that she's running.

A better man would demand to know her secrets and offer his protection freely. I'm quickly discovering that I'm not a good man. Not when it comes to Willow. I'll marry her. I'll protect her. I'll never let her go.

"What made you decide to marry a mail order bride?" Willow asks as I drive down Main.

It's a fair question and one I expected early on in our online chats, but it never came up. Neither did her reasoning for wanting to become a mail order bride.

"There aren't a lot of women in Crescent Ridge and most of the women you'll meet came here to marry men they met on Pearl's website," I tell her.

"Okay," she says. "But you could have met someone in Bramble, you're not mean or unattractive."

I snort at her reply.

"Women don't want to be with a man who can't even plan a date," I reply.

She opens her mouth to reply but snaps it closed when she glances at me. Something in my expression stops her and makes her sit back in the seat for a moment as my truck ambles along the paved two-lane road.

"You have anxiety?" she finally asks when I pull the truck into a parking space near the courthouse.

"Yes," I reply, my voice coming out strong but inside I'm a bundle of nerves.

This is it. She knows my weakness and she'll call this entire event off. She'll find another man wandering around the town and be swept off her feet and married before the day is over. There are enough mountain men and beefy lumberjacks who are single for her to have her pick of the bunch, and each one would commit murder to have the chance to marry a woman as beautiful as Willow. I'll be alone in my house just like I suspected when I drove down to Bramble this morning.

"I'm bossy," Willow says in a confiding whisper. "None of my past relationships liked how controlling I was. They said I was too picky."

I don't tell her what I think of the men in her past. They're all fools but that doesn't matter. If a single one had realized how special Willow is then she wouldn't be riding shotgun in my truck right now. Their mistakes have given me the opportunity of a lifetime to marry the sweetest woman I've ever met.

As bossy and demanding as she may be, her voice is soft and kind. Even now she's giving me an out when I know she needs my protection. Sweet as sugar and more understanding than I could ever hope. And she's all mine.

"Give me an itinerary every day if you like. Tell me when and where and I'll show up for you every time," I tell her.

The way her eyes light up tell me I've done something right. We sit in comfortable silence our eyes locking as we drink each other in

Her eyes dart to the clock on the dash, widening when she sees the time. She scurries out of the truck before I can even get my seatbelt unbuckled let alone around the truck to open her door.

"We're going to be late!" she shouts as I follow her up the stone steps leading up to the courthouse.

I don't comment that we're ten minutes early. Willow made it clear in her messages that she values punctuality. I made sure I arrived an hour earlier than her flight was due to land, not wanting to chance missing Willow's arrival.

I catch her elbow just before she makes it to the front door. She looks up at me in confusion but when I step forward to open the door, she adopts a sheepish expression. Her hand grabs mine and our clasped hands stay entwined the short walk to the clerk's office.

By the time our appointment rolls around we are standing in front of the judge who is pronouncing us husband and wife.

"You may kiss the-" the judge starts to say but I beat him to the punch.

My lips press gently against Willow's as she melts into my arms. If the judge says anything else, I don't hear a single word. Kissing my wife for the first time steals the breath from my body and sends my heart into race mode. I can't think with her in my arms. Her lips slide against mine breathing life into me and all I can focus on is her. There is no room for overthinking, just her and me. I hold onto her like she's the buoy in the storm of my life, until she pulls away.

Cheeks crimson and pupils wide, she stares at me unblinking. Her green eyes hold me captive as the judge mutters to himself.

"Newlyweds," the judge says as he shakes his head.

"My wife," I say to Willow.

Her eyes light with understanding. It all feels real now. I'm married. For the first time I feel anchored. Like I'm exactly where I'm meant to be. My entire life has led to this moment. Every wrong turn, every mistake led me right here. To this town and to this woman. To my Willow.

"My husband," she replies with a smile brighter than the fluorescent lighting above us.

This is it. This is us. For better or worse our lives are now fully intertwined. And I wouldn't have it any other way.

Willow

Corey's home-my home is a wonder to behold. He has flower beds filled with wildflowers around the house, no neatly trimmed hedges, or rock gardens. They are wild and untamed with blue and purple flowers bursting from long stalks.

"They're native to the area," Corey tells me when I comment on them. "Easier to grow and it helps out the bees."

Helps out the bees. I could melt into a puddle right here. My husband cares about the bees and native plants. He's a firefighter with anxiety, a soft smile that hints at a vulnerable and loving soul, and dark eyes that lead me straight into temptation.

This is a man I would have chosen for myself before my father died. Guilt twists my stomach and my heart beats erratically as Corey shows me our home. He goes pink any time he addresses the assortment of knickknacks that cover every available surface. This isn't a home plucked from the pages of a magazine. It's a real home with warmth and personality pouring out from every corner.

A place that under different circumstances would make me feel welcome and at ease only serves to make me feel like a fraud.

"I don't have a bed in the guestroom," Corey says pulling me from my thoughts as he shows me the master. "So you can take the bed, and I'll sleep on the couch until you're comfortable-"

"No," I say immediately. "We're married, and we'll sleep in the same bed."

I didn't expect this to be a paper marriage. As wrong as it feels to use Corey's name to protect myself it feels worse to even consider a platonic marriage. I might have started this marriage under false pretenses, but I will not let it be anything less than real from this point on. I owe Corey that much. I owe myself the same. Today was the happiest day of my life and I refuse to let guilt or insecurity cast their shadow over it.

"If you're sure," Corey says in a mild tone.

His voice is steady but his eyes pulse with a need so dark and dangerous I can barely endure his gaze. I don't verbally respond. I can't. This moment is too important to risk saying the wrong thing. To risk a misunderstanding.

Stepping forward I let my hands drift to the buttons of his green flannel shirt. The little bits of white plastic slide easily against the soft fabric as one by one I unbutton them. Corey stands still as a statue as I remove his shirt. The only visual response to my touch is the noticeable bulge stiffening behind the zipper of his pants.

Corey's eyes lock on to my face, barely blinking, as if he's afraid I'll disappear if he looks away for even a millisecond.

"You don't have-" he begins to say but cuts off his words midsentence when I send him a sharp look.

I know I don't have to. This man would never force my hand. He's the opposite of every grungy mechanic or biker I've ever dated. No dirty jokes or heavy-handed hints about how pretty my mouth would look with something in it. He's been a complete gentleman and that is the hottest thing.

Never mind the soft smiles and muscles. The man may look like a Roman god chiseled from marble but he's sweeter than spun sugar.

"I know," I say. "It's just all I've been thinking about since I saw you."

"Is that right?" he asks as my hands go to his belt.

"Well," I admit. "Ever since you referenced the itinerary."

His eyebrows climb as I unbutton his jeans and slide down his zipper.

"The itinerary?" he asks incredulously. "That's what got you all hot and bothered?"

Fingers poised to pull down his boxers and finally see his cock and I stop with an exasperated huff.

"Is this really what you want to talk about?" I ask him, raising one of my own eyebrows in turn.

We don't need to discuss how sexy I find it that he listened to me. That he took me seriously.

"No."

"Good," I reply tartly. "Because I would like to get to know my husband better. Starting with anatomy."

He cracks a grin as I sink to my knees in front of him. My hands wrap around his cock running up the length with smooth strokes. The grin fades as I tease his cock.

Running my tongue up the underside of his shaft draws a shaky breath from the man standing above me. His eyes are impossibly dark, nearly black, as they peer down at me. I don't look away as I take him into my mouth. The heavy weight of him on my tongue grounds me as I begin to slide up and down his length. The low moans the wet warmth of my mouth drags from him toe the line between guttural and primal.

I watch through heavy lashes as he loses himself. Making such a strong man weak in the knees sends a rush of power through my veins. Hollowing my cheeks I enjoy the way his thighs tremble underneath my nails as I drag them down to his knees.

"W-Willow," he groans between gritted teeth.

I continue unbothered.

"I'm not go-going to last," he bites out finally, but I ignore his protest.

I want to see him fall apart. See what he looks like at the height of passion. With my heartbeat pounding between my thighs, I don't think it'll take much for both of us to come right here.

"Willow. I don't want to come in your mouth the first time," he groans in a pleading tone.

Too bad I'm not feeling particularly merciful.

Corey

My wife is a different sort of wicked. This is far better than anything I could have imagined for our wedding night. From the second I accepted Willow's proposal I planned to give her space. I wanted her to be completely comfortable and settled in before we progressed our physical relationship. Now I feel like a fool for thinking we would ever spend the night apart.

The sight of her kneeling between my feet with her pert mouth wrapped around my cock is something I'll never forget.

"Holy-" I begin to say before my phone starts ringing.

My head tips back as I groan for a completely different reason than the one wrapped around my cock.

"Important call?" Willow asks as she lets go of my cock with a wet popping sound.

I frown down at her as I tuck myself back into my boxers and pull my jeans up. It's not my personal cell phone that's ringing. It's my work phone and there's only one reason it's ringing.

"There's a fire and they need backup," I tell Willow before I snatch up my phone and answer the call.

"Peters," I say trying to keep my tone even despite the untimely interruption.

"Wildfire," Captain Thomas states. "Finch estate on the west border of the national park. I need all hands on this one."

"On my way," I say before hanging up.

I turn to my wife ready to explain that I have to go despite it being our wedding day, but she's gone. I glance around but I don't see any sign of her.

"Willow!" I yell, hoping like hell she'll hear me and understand why I have to leave her alone on her first day in our home. "I have to go!"

I dart out the front door with a grimace but skid to a stop on the porch when I see Willow tossing her suitcase out the back of my truck.

"I cleaned it out!" she hollers when she looks up and sees me. "I'll be here when you're done."

My wife runs up to me before I can move a single step. She balances on her toes as she leans against my chest with an expectant look on her face.

"Kiss goodbye?" she asks when I hesitate a beat too long.

My lips slam against hers as my control slips. The wet slide of her lips on mine sends another pulse of desire to my cock and I nearly curse as I pull away. We've only barely begun, and I already have to leave before either of our desires are sated.

"I'll be back as soon as I can," I tell her before pressing another kiss to her pink lips.

"You'll be back when the job is done," Willow corrects. "I'll be here."

I gesture to her luggage as I climb into the truck cab.

"Get started on unpacking." I say through the open window. "Move anything you like. It's half yours."

I wave goodbye and drive off in a cloud of dust. I see Willow waving goodbye in the rearview mirror until I drive around a bend in the road. Halfway to the fire and I start kicking my own ass for not actually telling her goodbye. It's only as I approach the scene that I'm finally able to focus on the job ahead of me and not on the wife I've left at home.

Parking behind the firetruck I slip into my gear as fast as I can.

"Peters you're on pipe!" Captain Thomas orders when I run up.

I take over for Joe on the hose. My brain turns off and I become just another cog in the wheel as we battle the flames. Two properties border the national park on this side and Gunther Finch is the unlucky son of a bitch whose barn caught fire. With dry grass in his pasture, the fire caught and spread before he could react.

His barn is toast but it's no longer burning, white smoke curls into the sky while we continue trying to smother the flames still burning.

Sirens herald the arrival of the sheriff while I spray the base of the fire with almost three hundred PSI of water. The Carmichael brothers are already on the scene. Officially the three of them are not firefighters.

They work as lumberjacks for the local mill, but they grew up on this mountain and they're as committed as we are to protecting it. Any time a wildfire breaks out they get a call, and they come out with their chainsaws, and they help form a fire break.

It takes hours before the captain declares the site safe. The Carmichael's are covered in ash and sawdust and the rest of us are no better. I'm dog tired and all I want to do is take a shower and crawl into bed.

When I pull into the driveway it's pitch-black dark outside, and Willow has turned the porch light on. The house is quiet when I walk inside. Everything in the house looks the same as when I left. I wouldn't know my wife was even in our home if I didn't smell the food cooking in the kitchen.

"Bless you," I say under my breath when I step into the kitchen.

I linger just in the doorway watching my wife like I didn't just work a spontaneous call for several hours. Exhaustion and anxiety melt away as I stare like a lovestruck fool at the blonde pixie dancing around our kitchen.

Her back is to me, the strings of her apron tied around her waist in a bow so that it sits right above the waist of her jeans. She's changed clothing and her hair is slightly damp, the blonde strands a few shades darker than they were this afternoon.

I stare at her as she shifts from side-to-side humming off key. Our first day didn't start off too smoothly but as I watch her move around the kitchen like she's lived here every day of her life I know the next day is going to be better.

Moving into the space, I clear my throat and watch her startle at the sound. Her wooden spoon drops into the pot on the stove. Willow whirls around pulling out her earbuds as she does.

"Corey!" she shouts waving a hand to beckon me forward. "Come try a bite."

I reach for my wife as soon as I get close, but she thwarts me by shoving a spoon ladled with a white soup into my mouth. Potato and cream bursts on my tongue and I can see by the glint in her eye she knows just how good her cooking is.

"Could use some pepper," I grumble just to needle her a bit.

She huffs but her irritation melts a second later when I kiss her.

"It needs nothing," she says when I pull away swatting me on my chest as she does.

"No, it's perfect," I agree as she ladles a portion into a bowl for me.

I've barely sat down at the kitchen table before a timer goes off and she whips twin pans of freshly baked bread out of the oven with a set of mitts that match the pattern on her apron.

It's all I can do not to inhale the food. Especially when she hands me slices of warm bread. Willow looks on with pleased eyes as I help myself to a second bowl. The silence between us is comfortable, only broken by the clinking of spoons against bowls. Another time I would be trying to carry on a conversation with my bride. Find out every little detail that makes her who she is. When I'm bone sore and starved I can barely remain upright in my chair.

"Perfect," I tell her earnestly when I finish eating. "Absolutely perfect."

Her face lights up at my praise and if I weren't covered in grey ash from head to toe, I wouldn't hesitate to haul her off to our bedroom. As it is I need to wash up before I touch her again. I've already left a smudge on her cheek and added dirt to the flour on her apron.

"Shower?" she asks when I'm done.

If I weren't absolutely filthy, I might take offense from the way her nose scrunches up when she looks at my ashy clothes. As it is I stifle a laugh. This is far from the dirtiest I've been coming back from a fire fight.

"Join me?" I ask despite knowing that she's already showered.

I don't expect her to agree, I just want to tease her.

"I'll wash your back." she says before standing up from the table.

I watch as she moves around the kitchen. She tidies as I sit flummoxed by her casual agreement. After a moment she peers at me from over one delicate shoulder and raises a brow as her eyes scan the length of my body.

"I'm giving you a head start," she says.

When I don't move at her behest, she shoos be out of the kitchen by flapping a tea towel at me like a whip. Her laughter trails me to the bathroom, and I'm not surprised to see a wide smile in the mirror when I glance above the sink.

Turns out that marrying a mail order bride is silly indeed. And the best decision I've ever made in my adult life.

Willow

I hear the shower turn on and I rush to finish washing the dishes. The man is covered in soot from head to toe and smells like a bonfire. He needs a second to get a *little* bit cleaner before I join him. But I don't want to wait too long and miss the show.

We're married and I don't see any reason to be shy about letting him see my naked body or about ogling his. I've already seen his cock. I was tempted to finish what we started together while he was gone but it didn't feel as good when I tried. My fingers couldn't match the pleasure I felt watching him coming undone with my mouth wrapped around his cock.

Despite already showering I'm eager to get wet and soapy with the man who makes my knees tremble.

When I step into the bathroom the mirror is fogged over and there is steam pouring over the shower door. I can see the blurry outline of Corey's body moving through the transparent glass. Even with the steam obscuring most of his body my mind has no problem filling in the blanks.

I set a new speed record stripping off my clothes in my rush to join him. I hesitate right after I open the door, a warm billowing cloud of steam blowing past me as I see every wet soapy inch of him.

Hairy calves lead to thighs that are thick with corded muscle, an ass that flexes under my gaze, and a broad back with wide shoulders. He isn't as tall or broad as some of the men I've seen parading around the town of Crescent Ridge but the men in Chicago can't compare to the man in front of me.

And if I'm honest, none of the other men in Crescent Ridge can either. The way water sluices and drips off every contour of his muscles has me dripping a different type of liquid down my thighs.

He drags a cloth covered in blue tinted soap across his chest as he turns to find me staring at him unabashed. The grin that spreads across his face is filled with masculine pride and raw hunger.

"Like what you see?" he asks.

The cloth dips lower and my eyes twitch with eagerness to follow its trail but Corey's dark gaze holds me enraptured. I know what lies at the end of that path. I've seen it. I've tasted it.

"Yes," I reply.

Stepping into the shower I close the door behind me, enclosing us in a heated bubble of damp air that clings to my skin. Corey's body slides against mine coating me in minty bubbles as his chin dips down and he pulls me in for a kiss.

There's not a spot of my body that his hands leave untouched. The fire his touch ignites burns hotter than the water pouring down on us from the rainfall shower head.

"I want to taste you," he whispers into the shell of my ear.

His hands roam my waist squeezing my hips before sliding around to grab my ass. Our lips meet as his hands squeeze my cheeks in pulses. Tongues duel in lazy strokes and my hands stay busy exploring his torso, the muscles under my fingers tensing under my touch.

"Later," I whisper in reply.

It's only been a few hours, but it feels like I've been waiting all day for my husband to come home. I wasn't waiting all that time for his tongue. I'm more than ready to consummate this marriage fully.

I see Corey begin to protest but something he must see in my expression stops him. The pad of his thumb catches on my bottom lip as he stares down at me with a thoughtful look.

"Want my cock that badly?" he asks.

I don't answer verbally. I nod my head in response.

"Then you'll get it," he growls. "Any way you want it, as often as you want it."

My hands scramble for purchase on his shoulders when he uses his grip on my ass to lift me up against the tile wall. The white subway tile is cold but with Corey between my thighs I'm unbothered by the chill at my back.

"Aren't you agreeable?" I murmur. "And eager?"

I arch into his body as he nibbles at my neck, his breath hotter than the steam swirling around us.

"For you?" he replies. "Always."

The hard line of his cock presses between us, the rounded tip resting against my belly button. With his body pining mine to the wall, his hands are free to wander. Over my thighs, his thumbs skating along the inner flesh while his fingers stroke the outer. Then up my stomach to my breasts, his large palms dwarfing them.

Heat pools between my thighs the evidence of my arousal dripping down to the floor as he toys with my nipples.

"So responsive..." Corey murmurs as his fingers stroke the hardened nubs.

"For you," I reply breathlessly. "Always."

My moans echo in the confined space, every kiss, every touch, pulling another from somewhere deep in my chest. By the time Corey pulls back I don't recognize the wanton woman he's made me. He slides into me with ease, my pussy slick and welcoming as he pushes his hips forward slowly. For all my clawing encouragement he takes his time, sinking into me inch by inch until I've taken it all.

The girth stretches me to my limit, the fullness soothing some frayed edge deep inside me. His first few thrusts are shallow and slow, his dark caramel eyes locked on me seeking any discomfort or hesitation. His hold on my hips is so tight I can't buck against him, can't force him to hurry or give me more than he's allowing.

Mindless frustration builds until I'm begging.

"Faster," I order, digging my heels into the base of his spine.

He pauses with the tip of his cock just barely resting inside my pussy.

"No," he says with a smirk.

Resuming his slow pace, he ignores my heels drumming against his ass in retaliation. I know he wants more. I can see it in the way he tenses his shoulders. The way he grips my thighs to the point I know I'm going to wake up with finger shaped bruises.

He's infuriating, and he knows it. The damn bastard is smug about it.

"Please," I cry as he shifts his hips and hits a spot that has me gasping as tingles race down my spine.

It's like a live wire is connecting the most sensitive points all over my body. The electrical current racing between them has my pussy spasming around his cock in a shallow imitation of an orgasm.

"Hm," he hums in reply. "You won't let me taste you, but you'll order me to fuck you. How is that fair?"

My head slams back into the wall behind me but I don't feel the pain. I'm on edge, every shallow thrust of his hips is pushing me closer. I need more. I need it hard and fast. I want to dive off the edge in a breathless crescendo, not slip off gently on a cloud.

"Taste me later," I whisper, tilting my head down to look at the man driving me to madness. "Fuck me now."

"So, bossy," he whispers back, his grin wide. "You know most men don't like having a wife who bosses them around."

From another man it would be a criticism. From Corey, it's a compliment.

"Not you," I say just as he slams his hips against mine.

My next words are stolen from my lungs as he begins pounding into me like a man possessed. The look in his eyes is feral as he chases our high, pulling me along with him on a frantic quest to see who falls apart first.

I watch him as he watches me. Our gazes darting down briefly to where we're joined, his cock driving into my pussy mercilessly as the sounds of our bodies meeting surrounds us. Each sound obscene. Every thrust divine.

Our breathing mingles as we both gasp for air, the shower still pouring warm water down on us. A bead of water on his chest distracts me for a second and Corey darts forward to nip my lip in reproach.

"Eyes on mine, wife," he growls, as his hips punch into mine with more force than before.

It's enough to have me scoring his shoulders with my nails, my head thrown back and my voice shouting his name as I come apart in his arms. My inner muscles milk his cock like they're pulling his soul from his body, and he tenses as his seed splashes into me coating my walls in thick warm spurts. Each one sends another tremor through my body, one aftershock on top of another until he slumps against me catching his breath.

We don't separate until the water runs cool. My legs unsteady, Corey keeps a firm grip on me as we finish washing in contented silence. It's not until we're sliding into the massive California king size bed that dominates our bedroom that I break that silence.

"Well, that wasn't on the itinerary," I say causing Corey to chuckle as he wraps his body around mine.

"It should be," he says as we settle down to sleep. "Every single day."

My heart trips at his words. The effortless way he accepts me and all my routines. It's barely been a day, but I know that I'm already falling for my husband. He'll have my heart before winter, and it cuts me deeply that I'll always have this secret buried in my past.

Corey deserves better but I'm too selfish to let him go.

Corey

Married life suits me well. Nearly a month of marriage and I don't see the honeymoon phase fading anytime soon. I love my wife with every fiber of my being. She stole my heart that first day and every day after has only reinforced her claiming. She's supportive of my career even when it interferes with other aspects of our lives. Being a firefighter's wife isn't for the weak, but Willow has adapted admirably. She doesn't complain or cry when I have to leave on a call. She never fails to kiss me goodbye and welcome me home after each call.

Willow has made her mark on my heart, and I want to shout it from the rooftops.

I haven't told her yet because I don't want to chase her away. She's still gun shy from something in her past. I see the shadows in her eyes from time to time.

Occasionally, she starts to say something before choking on her words and changing the subject to something else. I won't be able to hold back my feelings for much longer, already I think she can see it in my eyes, feel it in my touch.

Most nights we have sex. The nights we don't lead to mornings that we spend tangled in bed together. If I could read her mind as easily as I read her body, I could reassure her that I have her back no matter what trouble is chasing her.

As it is I do everything within my ability to show her that I love her. That I cherish her. I follow her itineraries like a GPS. I readjust all my routines to compliment hers.

I even fold my socks now.

Nothing is too small, too outlandish. I don't care if a shirt is folded horizontally or vertically but Willow does. So, I fold the correct way.

The Willow way.

If she could see the way her name is stamped across my heart she would understand. Sometimes I see her looking at me the way I know I look at her. Her heart on display as clearly as mine. But we don't talk about our feelings.

It's too soon.

My buddies all laughed and slapped my back when I introduced Willow to them. They called me a lovestruck fool and offered their sincerest condolences to my bride. She took their jokes all in stride. Even told Bill that he would have to find a blind woman willing to marry him with all his red flags.

They love her. I even caught two of them using the mail order bride app on their phones at lunch. And the other mail order brides married to firemen, Gloria and Alisa, love her too.

They have a standing brunch date on Sundays now.

It's early one morning when I'm making Willow breakfast that I hear a car pull into the gravel driveway. It's the first time I've beaten my wife into the kitchen since she moved in. I don't want her thinking that I'm helpless and that she always needs to cook.

I'm sure it's one of my buddies until the pounding knocks rattle the door frame. It's a cop knock. A glance out the window on my way to the front door reveals a black SUV rather than the sheriff's truck.

No local would drive anything without four-wheel drive. I grumble about lost travelers with rude manners the last few steps to the oak door.

"I'm here for Willow Peters," the man says when I open the door.

No greeting, just straight to business. I can respect it even if his tone irks me.

"Why?" I ask.

His eyes are hidden behind dark sunglasses and the mouth below is neither smiling nor frowning. Something about him raises the hairs on the back of my neck. Maybe it's his posture, ramrod straight as if he's not entirely human. Or maybe it's the black suit in the middle of July in Crescent Ridge. It's too hot for black. It's too hot for a suit. And there is nowhere close he would be expected to wear one.

This guy is bad news and he's looking for my wife.

"Does it matter?" he asks.

When I don't deign to answer he sighs before removing his sunglasses.

"She's not worth it," he tells me as he puts his glasses into his pocket.

"Yes, she is," I growl.

He's built like a hockey enforcer, large in the shoulders and thighs with massive hands that look like they can cause damage. The scarring on his knuckles is telling enough that I don't want to fight this man. But if he's a threat to my wife then it's inevitable.

"She owes the Carrisi family a large sum of money."

Chicago sharks. A mafia family with a terrifying reputation and I count myself lucky that I didn't try to fight the man in front of me. Even if I took him out three more goons would pop up to replace him.

"How much?"

He raises an eyebrow. My own rises to match. I want this man gone and the fastest way to make that happen is to pay him the money.

"One hundred thousand."

His dark eyes appraise me, and I see him pause his perusal in two places. At the hole in the knee of my jeans, worn from use and not for style, and at my watch. It was my grandfather's and while it's not worth a hundred thousand dollars it does have some value.

Enough value that I can see the cogs in his mind whirling. He's wondering if I can pay Willow's debt.

"I need to make a phone call," I tell him.

I start to close the door in his face when his foot strikes out preventing it from moving further.

"Cops won't help you," he tells me.

He stares at me with a dark look in his eyes that I'm sure is supposed to be menacing. He doesn't know our local sheriff, or he wouldn't make such a claim. Our local law enforcement is made up of good people but that's not who I'm going to call, and I tell him so.

"Lawyers can't help either," he replies.

He crosses his arms and stands belligerently in my door frame.

"Not. Who. I'm. Calling," I bite out.

He leans forward into my space, and I'm tempted to throw a punch at his jaw. But the thought that this man could hurt Willow is the only logic I need to keep my hands complacently at my sides.

"Who?" he asks.

"Boris Kuznetsov," I reply.

I don't use his moniker. The light that sparks in this thug's eyes tells me he knows the name. And exactly how much weight it holds.

"The Rook isn't going to war with the Carrisi's over a woman," he says.

I think about the man who owes me a favor. He's arguably worse than every member of the Carrisi family combined. And this grunt in front of me is correct. Boris Kuznetsov would never risk war for a woman.

"No," I agree. "But he will cover the debt."

"You don't look like a made man," he says more to himself than me.

He scans me from head to toe again, no doubt searching for a clue that I'm a retired assassin or enforcer for the Russian Mafia.

"I'm not," I reply in a bored tone. "Now, let me make a call so your boss can get his money."

This time when I move to shut the door he moves out of the way. I don't take out my cell phone until I see him walk back to his car. His phone is already in his hand and I'm sure that he's calling to inform his boss about the new development.

The smell of burning bacon hits my nose before I can find the right contact in my phone.

"Fuck," I mutter dashing back to the kitchen before I burn my own cabin down.

"Corey?" Willow calls out as she steps out of our bedroom.

She's wearing a tank top and a pair of tiny silk sleep shorts that fry my brain instantly. With her short blonde hair all rumpled, sticking out straight in places, she looks like an angry cockatoo ruffling it's feathers to make itself appear larger. That hair looks the same way when I card my fingers through it during sex and with her eyes still heavy with sleep, I'd love nothing more than to take her right back to bed.

But this isn't any other morning.

"We had a visitor," I tell her.

I need to distract myself before I act on my urges instead of addressing the problem in front of us.

The way Willow's eyes dart to mine is telling. I knew she was running from something. Now I know what it was.

"Enforcer for the Carrisi family," I answer her unspoken question.

"I wanted to tell you," she says. "I swear. I just-"

She stops abruptly and I notice the way her eyes shine when she looks away from me. Her shoulders tremble and I hear the soft hitch in her breath. I don't need to see or hear anything more. I won't let her think this affects our relationship.

"You were scared."

It's not a question but she nods anyway.

"My dad had a gambling problem, and I didn't know until they came to collect his debt after the funeral," she explains with her voice shaking.

I didn't need an explanation. Willow isn't the type to fall prey to the Carrisi's of her own volition. Even if she were I wouldn't care. It couldn't change the way I love her. When I open my arms for her, she slumps against my chest. By this weekend, this problem will be ancient history but for now I can almost feel the weight of her fear crushing her. The way she burrows her button nose in my chest breaks my heart.

"I'll take care of it."

Her sage green eyes are glassy when she looks up at me from wet eyelashes. The doubt is clear in her expression, but I'm not offended by her lack of faith. Without a favor owed by Kuznetsov I wouldn't be able to make this situation go away. I have savings but nothing close to what her father owed the family. That they would force her to repay his debt is beyond infuriating. Taking advantage of an innocent woman like this is cruelty at its most basic level.

"It's too much money, Corey," Willow says.

Her voice is raspy and meek as it comes from the folds of my shirt that her fists have bunched up.

"I have it handled," I tell her.

I press her against my chest and despite her grumbles she squeezes me back tightly in response.

Willow

Two hours after my past came to collect, Corey leads me to the living room where a laptop is balanced on our coffee table. A large man wearing a suit despite looking like he'd be more comfortable in a boxing ring stands behind the table with his hands clasped behind his back.

Corey's warm hand guides me to the couch and with a gentle tug he pulls me down to sit beside him. Our legs touch from knee to hip and his arm wraps around me surrounding me with his presence and easing the tension in my body as his vanilla and cinnamon scent covers me like a warm blanket.

Once we're seated the enforcer opens a video call connection and resumes his post. His dark eyes staring at us unblinking.

"Mrs. Peters," a svelte man greets me through the screen.

Short blonde hair neatly combed back without a strand out of place and the tailored three-piece suit give away his identity immediately. I've never met him in person but everyone in Chicago knows who runs their city.

He resembles a panther with how easily he lounges in his chair like a predator watching a mouse try to scramble out of his hold. His long legs are crossed at the knee and his hand that rests on the arm of his ornate armchair is adorned with a single ring.

Edward Carrisi.

"Mr. Carrisi," I reply.

I ignore the way my voice shakes when I greet the head of the largest crime family in the country. He's younger than I expected but I can see the cruel glint in his eyes and in his smile.

"You inherited a large debt from your father," he begins. "Truly an impressive amount for a middle-class woman."

I remain silent. There is nothing for me to say. I can't deny that my father racked up the debt. All I can do is wait for this man to decide my fate.

"Smart of you to run, although it's bad for business," he murmurs. "Sending my men to chase after a young woman wasn't a good look for the organization, you understand? Especially when you were able to get out of the city undetected. Steven is going to need some retraining."

The man standing behind the laptop is unable to hide his wince, and I wonder if his name is Steven. Or if the enforcer who broke into my apartment is the one in hot water.

A man off camera offers Mr. Carrisi a glass with amber liquid and the don takes a sip before waving the man away.

"You're lucky, Mrs. Peters," he says eyes pinning me in place. "Lucky that your husband has friends in the right places. And lucky that I want this entire debacle to be done."

He looks over his shoulder when a loud ping echoes through the room.

"Got it, Boss," says the man off screen.

"Our business is concluded Mrs. Peters," he says with a smile every bit as menacing as before. "Congratulations on your marriage."

The screen goes black before I can formulate a reply.

Steven or not-Steven snaps the laptop closed and leaves us without a word spoken.

I turn to look at my husband, a wave of relief easing the tension from my shoulders. I stare at the man I married and for the first time I feel like I'm looking at a stranger. Dozens of questions burn through my brain but as I stare at the man who holds my heart in the palm of his hand, I can only ask one.

"How?" The word is quiet, barely more than a whisper.

"It's a long story but the short of it is that I saved a bad man's life a long time ago when I lived in Denver. As a firefighter I save everyone. Doesn't matter in the least what kind of person they are. A life is a life. But he didn't see it that way. Figured he owed me a favor for saving his life and every so often he checks in with me."

I stare at Corey in disbelief.

"When I found out about the debt I called in that favor."

I shouldn't ask. But I do. I have to know who could be powerful enough to wipe my debt clean and call off Carrisi's enforcers.

"Who?" I ask.

Corey audibly swallows before he answers.

"The Rook."

"You were owed a favor by *The Rook*, and you wasted it on me?" I ask incredulously.

"I didn't waste it," Corey says his color returning as his face flushes with anger. "He felt like he owed me. He didn't but he wanted to even the scales. And my wife was in trouble so of course I asked him to settle the matter."

The Rook. The kingpin of Denver. Arguably the only man more terrifying and ruthless than Edward Carrisi. I don't even know his name. I just know his nickname and rank. The bratva pakhan.

"Thank you," I say.

It's not everything I want to convey. Hell, it barely brushes the surface. Corey married me without knowing about my debt to the Italian mafia. And when he found out he handled it. He didn't yell or accuse me of tricking him. By all rights it would be completely understandable if he asked for a divorce. Or an annulment, I guess since we haven't been married a full month yet.

But his dark eyes don't hold anger in their brown depths. The caramel swirls still sparkle brilliantly when I gaze into them. He looks at me the same way he did yesterday and the day before. The same way he's looked at me since we met in that airport lobby.

Like he treasures me.

"Corey-" I begin, I have to tell him how I feel, how much he means to me. "I-"

"I love you, Willow," he says beating me to the punch. "I'd do anything for you. If he didn't owe me a favor, I would have borrowed the sum from him."

Hot anger courses through me just thinking of my husband being indebted to the Russian Mafia. Not to save me. Corey is a good man and the thought of him being at their mercy, forced to sacrifice his morals turns my stomach with dread.

"No!" I shout. "Not for me!"

"Yes!" Corey shouts back. "You're my wife! Of course, for you!"

Tears fall from my eyes cutting warm paths down my cheeks as I stare up at my husband.

"I love you too," I tell him. "I was literally about to tell you when you interrupted me."

The smile he wears is soft but a teensy bit smug.

"I know," he says. "That's why I did it."

Epilogue

Corey

I smell the soup before I open the front door. With the dead of winter hitting the mountain hard this year, Willow has taken to making soups, stews, and casseroles with relish. I have the same zeal about eating everything she makes.

For all the men who worry about their wives adapting to small town life and the harsh realities of living on the mountain I never had the same concerns with Willow. She took to mountain life with ease, mingling with locals like she was born here. A month after she moved in, she answered a job posting at the local daycare. It's a far cry from the factory that she used to work at but a welcome one.

"It'll be good practice," she said when I told her she didn't need to work.

I allowed those words to stew in my mind for all of a day before I asked her to take a pregnancy test. She made me wait another two weeks before she finally took the one I bought the day I suspected.

She just smiled indulgently while I paced the length of our bedroom the entire three minutes we had to wait.

My keys land on the hook next to hers, same with my coat and boots. Everything that used to be a single has become one of a mix matched pair in this house. After we resolved the debt with Carrisi, Willow and I went back to her apartment to box up the rest of her stuff. Since she was running from the mafia, she didn't cancel her lease or tell anyone that she was moving. All her belongings were right where she left them. All the figurines from the anime shows that she likes. All the books and manga too.

When she moved in, she insisted that it was all just material possessions that could be replaced with time, but she couldn't hide the pleased blush when we went back for her things.

We've commissioned more shelves from Liam so that we can display more of her collectibles. As it is her knick-knacks and mine war for space on every surface. All I see as I walk through our home are signs of my wife loving our home and our life here.

"Potato?" I ask as I step into the kitchen.

Willow already has two steaming bowls ready on the table.

"Your nose is on a winning streak," she replies.

She's perfected dozens of recipes but her potato soup will always be my favorite because it was the first one she made for us. Every time we have it for dinner I'm taken back to that first night when I came home dirty and tired to a delicious hot meal made by my sweet wife.

I wait patiently as she shuffles around the kitchen. After a moment she notices me lingering by the table and smiles even as she huffs an exasperated breath my way.

"You don't have to wait for me," she says.

I ignore her protest as I hold out her chair. She knows I won't sit down to eat dinner until she's seated. Between my shifts at the fire station and Willow's work at the daycare we don't always get to share our meals at the same time.

"I'm not made of glass, Corey."

The phrase has become a common occurrence these last few months.

"I will not sit on my ass while my wife works around me letting her food get cold," I say waiting to eat my food until Willow takes her first bite.

The smile on her face is pleased, her cheeks pink as she eats her soup. She might huff and puff, she might protest and argue, but she enjoys the chivalry. More so now that her back aches and her feet are swollen. If I had it my way, she'd be on bedrest but both Willow and Dr. Winslow think I'm overreacting.

"Delicious as always," I compliment after a few bites.

"Doesn't need a dash of pepper?" she asks with a cheeky grin.

"Never."

Willow and I talk about our respective work as we eat. I spent a good portion of my day helping the newest probie wash the truck and Willow has taken over the seven-year-old group.

"Percy Hart is the ringleader." She confides. I help her ease into the recliner before sitting cross legged on the ground at her feet.

"What has Daniel's son done now?" I ask.

Last week it was roughhousing on the playground and the week before that he repeated a dirty joke he heard from his father. The fathers of the other kids in Percy's group are still teasing him about that one.

"He convinced the other boys that all the girls have cooties," Willow says as I grab her left foot, my thumbs rubbing the arch.

"Sounds innocent enough."

"Four girls cried," she says.

She recounts the preschool drama as I rub her feet until she's a melted puddle of bliss.

"At this point the other parents are never going to let the Hart's forget this," Willow says.

"None of their children are innocent little angels either," I reply as I move up from her foot to her ankle. "Ours will be the same."

"For sure," Willow agrees between moans. "Teacher's kids always act out."

The desk in the corner sits below a window that has a wonderful view of the mountain side in the afternoons. It's where Willow does her coursework for her online classes. She's on the fast track to earn her bachelor's degree in early childhood education. After she started working at the daycare she fell in love with working with children. The daily schedules and routines are like butter on a warm roll to her.

Not that her obsession with time management and scheduling is exclusive to her work by any means. Whenever we go on dates, Willow sets an itinerary on my phone, and I follow it to the letter.

"Joe's bride wants to talk about your courses. He said she's looking for an online school to get her degree in ornithology."

Willow mumbles something that sounds like agreement and I know she'll call Miranda tomorrow. Before she can get too comfortable, I urge her to stand. She sways on her feet, and I scoop her up before she can fall back into the chair. Her head rolls against my chest as I carry her into our bedroom. She is sound asleep when I slide her into the sheets.

I leave her to nap in peace as I return to the kitchen to clean up from dinner. Leftovers go into the fridge, and I wash the dishes before I return to my wife's side. She's barely moved an inch since I tucked her in to bed.

I slide into the bed and the moment that I lay my head down, Willow rolls over to cuddle against my side. It takes all of a second to have me wrapped in her arms. Not a day goes by that Willow doesn't seek my touch. She openly displays her affection, and it makes me love her just a little bit more.

Signing up for a mail order bride was the best decision I've ever made. It brought me Willow, the sweetest woman I've ever met, and our unborn child. I promised to love, cherish, and honor my wife six months ago, and I will uphold those vows until the day I take my last breath.

The End

Eager to meet Miranda and Joe? Read their love story that begins with her coming to Crescent Ridge to marry the wrong man and being left abandoned at a campsite near the summit in Mountain Man's Abandoned Mail Order Bride. No car, no cell phone, and no one knows her groom-to-be has left her stranded with a storm rolling in quickly.

***

You can sign up for my newsletter or follow me on Amazon or Facebook for updates on new releases and more.

Mountain Man's Abandoned Mail Order Bride

Jacqueline Carmine

Miranda

It's official. Men ruin everything. A month ago, I would have sworn that it was just the men in Boston. Every relationship stalled out and every set up or blind date was a poor match.

A weaker woman would blame herself.

I blame men.

I grew tired of watching my own relationships end in flames along with those of my friends. I blamed Boston men, which considering how Raymond ditched me might have been a tad overzealous.

Signing up with Pearl's Mail Order Brides after a pint of ice cream and a bottle of red might have been an impulsive decision. The first one of my life. I worked as an HR manager in the same city I was born in. I went to a local college, got a sensible business degree, and waited for Mr. Right.

Except he never arrived. Maybe he got lost on the way or snatched up by someone else. But as it stood, I decided to take my fate into my own hands and signed up for a match.

Raymond was good on paper. Successful contractor with a steady job and an upbeat look on love. He said he was looking for his soulmate. And I believed him.

Considering today's turn of events, I would say he is a liar.

I should have turned around at the airport and bought myself a ticket back home. Now I'm stranded on this fucking mountain and only have myself to blame. I took a chance on love and lost.

He met me at the gate. Not with flowers or a banner but with a big smile and a heated look. Grand gestures of love were not my fiancé's strong suit. I brushed my romantic notions aside. Hopeless romantic or not, I am a realist. I know men are not perfect. And while Raymond's actions and words fell short of my expectations, I told myself those standards were set too high.

I went with him, expecting us to go to his rental house but instead he proved he could surprise me.

"There is this great campsite near the peak," he told me as he tossed my luggage into the bed of his truck.

The pink case landed hard on the rusty metal bed next to a nylon tent bag and some other camping supplies and I couldn't hide my wince. Not that Raymond noticed.

"You're gonna love it babe," he said before he climbed into his truck cab.

I stood beside the passenger side door for a second. Contemplating how much of a scene I would cause by snatching my luggage out of his truck and marching myself back inside the airport. Then the passenger side door popped open, and my goodwill returned.

I assumed he was just nervous to be marrying a stranger.

"Camping for the honeymoon?" I asked even as I was mentally trying to get on board.

"No. No. No," he replied. "This is the last weekend before they close the campgrounds for the year. We have to go today, or we'll miss our chance!"

Looking down at my thin pink cotton sundress and wedge heels I found myself fighting for my typical cheery outlook. I liked to think of myself as an optimist. A practical optimist.

I wore my cutest dress because I thought I was meeting my future husband on the day of our wedding. I even wore makeup and styled my hair. I wanted to wear comfy clothes on the plane, but I decided it was more important to make a good first impression. I wasn't dressed for roughing it in the wilderness. Nor was I the type to enjoy the outdoors. But I didn't want to start my marriage off on the wrong foot by starting a fight.

On the way up the mountain from the airport in Bramble, I asked him a series of questions. Nothing too crazy.

What life as a traveling contractor was like and such. Feeling that I had broken the ice with the man I was set to marry I treaded into deeper waters.

"I thought we were getting married today," I said, trying to lead him into a discussion about how impractical and unsettling a spontaneous camping trip was for me.

"No point if we're not compatible, is there?" he replied like it was obvious.

I wanted to tell him that I didn't pack up my life and hop on a plane for a trial run. When he proposed, we agreed we would marry the same day I arrived. We talked for months and now he wants to see if we're compatible.

The impromptu camping trip did have an upside. Despite the inappropriate footwear I was able to catch sight of a pine grosbeak. A gorgeous bird in any right. Raymond didn't give a damn about the birds I spotted and that was another sign I tried valiantly to ignore.

He was the one who wanted to go camping but the only thing he wanted to do was have sex. Call me crazy, but a nylon tarp over rocky ground doesn't exactly scream sexy.

Two hours later, I would come back from a bathroom break–in the woods–to find the campsite empty and his truck gone. The only thing he left was my luggage. The pink case was left lying in the dirt.

All because I didn't want to have sex with him for the first time in a tent when I just got off a plane.

Asshole. Men are the worst. Boston. Crescent Ridge. They're all the same. A thick crack of thunder sends a chill rolling down my spine as goosebumps raise on my arms.

The sky overhead is dark, and the wind is picking up. That asshole left me stranded in an unfamiliar location with no shelter and a thunderstorm rolling through.

Head tilted to the sky I feel the first raindrop land on my cheek, and I open my mouth and let out the scream that's been clawing at my chest. Heart pounding, I scream loud enough to send animals scattering. It's raw and it's primal but once I let it out, I feel better.

I'm still stranded on a mountain in severe weather. But I'm still Miranda Garcia and I'm not going to sit on my ass and wallow. No one knows where I am besides Raymond and that means there is no chance of someone coming to find me.

With the rain falling faster and shifting from large raindrops to small stinging pellets I grab my luggage and get my butt into gear. Sundress plastered to my skin and wedges sinking deep into the dirt that is quickly becoming mud I set off.

Joe

"Help Darren check the campsites," Captain Thomas said. "Most are cleared but someone reported a truck with two occupants driving up the mountain this afternoon."

"On it," I replied.

I might be a firefighter but most of my time is spent doing anything but fighting fires. In Crescent Ridge we're not just part of the firefighting crew we're also the rescue team. We find stranded hikers. We lecture about fire safety, and we aid the park rangers as needed.

The storm is beginning to roll through as I drive up the mountain. Dark clouds block out the sun and the wind is strong enough to send the pine trees swaying and dancing. Around every corner of the climb, I can feel the wind hitting the sides of my truck and forcing me to make a correction to stay in my lane.

Surely there isn't anyone left on this mountain foolish enough to try to ride out this storm in a nylon tent.

I'm nearly to the turnoff for the first trailhead when I see someone walking alongside the road. Tall with light brown skin and curly dark hair that is as soaked as the pale pink sundress clinging to her curves is a woman who steals the breath from my chest. She's pulling a bright pink rolling suitcase behind her and from what I can tell through the heavy rain blanketing my windshield she looks about as happy as a wet cat.

In my haste, I nearly drove the truck into the ditch. Kicking myself for the near miss I don't let myself look at her again until I've brought the truck to a safe stop in the middle of the lane. With no safe spot to pull over on the narrow two-lane road I flip my hazards on before I throw the truck into park.

No one should be coming up this mountain anyway unless they're here to rescue this woman and my gut says no one is coming. She's not a local or I would recognize her.

Hopping out of the truck I'm drenched by the time I reach the mystery woman's side. Her eyes rake down my body and for a moment she is as enraptured by me as I am with her.

"What the hell are you doing?" I ask once I'm close enough for her to hear me. "Did you miss all the warnings to evacuate, or did you think they didn't apply to you?"

It's not what I meant to say. Instead of a polite introduction my mouth ran full steam ahead without input from my brain. Her dark almond eyes peer at me from thick lashes that are narrowed in anger. Just as I'm about to apologize and try to pull my foot out of my mouth she fires back.

"What does it look like I'm doing?" she asks with a snarl. "I'm walking down this infernal mountain."

"That's stupid," I reply. "It's at least an hour to town on foot, and the storm is only going to get worse."

"What was my other option?" she asks. "Huddle underneath a tree and pray I don't get struck by lightning or freeze to death?"

Her sharp tone has my cock hard and I'm hoping she doesn't notice. There's heat in those brown eyes but it's the wrong kind. And if she noticed the bulge in my jeans, it might just make her angrier.

"You could've stayed with your car," I tell her even as I wave her over to the truck.

She throws a suspicious look my way and I can see her calculating the risk of trusting a stranger. I point a finger to the logo on my shirt and then wave a hand toward the truck where the fire station's logo is printed on the side.

She follows me to the truck without a word and doesn't comment until I've opened the passenger door for her.

"I don't have a car," she tells me.

She brushes past without looking at me, her chin held high. Her pink luggage takes up most of the floorboard, but I don't offer to throw it in the back seat. Judging by her white knuckled grip on the handle I would have a better chance of taking a cub from a momma grizzly. After I shut her door, I discreetly adjust myself so that her effect on me isn't super obvious.

"How did you get up the mountain?" I ask when I join her in the cab.

No one called in to report a missing person or a stranded hiker. I checked three other campsites on my way up and one simple phone call would have streamlined this entire process. Whoever her friends are, they must not be worried about her safety. Seems like the type of thing a bunch of dumb college students would pull but she doesn't look like a student.

"I don't want to talk about it," she mutters as I drive.

Seeing her shiver, I turn on the heat in the truck. We're both soaked from the rain but while I wasn't in the downpour for more than ten minutes, she's been outside more than long enough to freeze.

"Are you really a firefighter?" she asks.

The question catches me off guard in the silence of the cab. I would think the answer would be obvious from the truck and my clothing, but I reply in the affirmative all the same.

"Most first responders I've met are more professional," she says.

I bite back a smile as she warms up to verbally berate me for my 'lackluster' rescue. This woman has fire, I'll give her that.

"I am normally *such* a nice and understanding sort of person. You have no idea. But you made me feel like an idiot even though it wasn't my fault I was stranded in this storm. Don't take out your little grumpy attitude on me!"

If it weren't for my jeans, my cock would smack against the steering wheel. Angry women have never turned me on before, and I'm fully unprepared. I can't think straight long enough to formulate a response to calm her down. So, she just keeps going as I sit there and take it in stride.

"I've had enough of men who think they know better than I do. I dealt with enough of that shit in Boston and I don't need it from you too! I'm a fucking adult and I know what's best for me!"

At some point I'm going to have to jump in and introduce myself. It's not every day that you meet the woman meant for you and I don't even know her first name. She's not wearing a wedding ring, but she will be soon. I knew it the second those dark eyes met mine. Even before she opened her mouth and let me have it from both barrels, I knew I had met my match.

"You can wipe that smirk off your face too," she adds without losing steam. "This isn't funny."

My chuckle fills the cab. Her face gets a delicious red tint to her cheekbones, and I can see her getting ready to yell at me again.

"It is a little funny," I tell her. "You don't even know my name, but you've already given me a dressing down that puts my mother's guilt trips to shame."

She's silent for a beat. An impressive feat considering how well she's carried the conversation without my help so far.

"What's your name?" she asks.

"Joe Kalinski," I tell her. "And what delightful little ray of sunshine did I pick up today?"

"Miranda Garcia," she replies. "And I *am* a ray of sunshine. Thank you very much. Today has just been exceptionally trying."

"Tell me about it."

"No, it's too much," she replies. "And far too embarrassing."

"I nearly drove my truck into a ditch trying to stop to help you," I say. "I think I deserve a little backstory."

Miranda

Naturally as soon as I declare all men bastards, I would meet the perfect man. Even if he was a jerk. Considering he didn't know the circumstances that led to me wandering the mountain road, his initial irritation was valid. Entirely unprofessional but valid all the same.

He let me yell at him as he drove us up the mountain to the closest turnaround spot. The very same campsite I had just left. Another man might have kicked me out of his truck, but Joe didn't. No, he didn't yell back or get snippy. He just sat there as I ranted and began to smile.

Which only pissed me off more. The man is already criminally good looking with his cowboy hat pulled low and his long brown beard shadowing his jaw. Everything about him screams man. He's nothing like the perfectly polished and overly groomed men I met in Boston. Even Raymond seems less masculine by comparison.

Our height difference is evident even in the confined space of the truck cab. I'm tall for a woman and I'm used to looking me in the eye, but he is a good bit taller than I am. When he stood next to me in the rain, I felt small in comparison. The top of his hat brushes the roof while I have a good foot of free space above my head. When he stepped out of the truck, and I saw him for the first time something went soft inside me.

I've known beautiful men. I've dated my fair share. But Joe was something else. Something about his broad shoulders and thick thighs sends heat spiraling through me despite the freezing rain and wind. I was ready to fall into his arms and straight into his bed. Never mind my swearing off all men thirty minutes before. No, for a man that ruggedly handsome, I was ready to make an exception.

Then he opened his mouth and ruined the moment. Now with my toes finally beginning to thaw and his warm leather and pine scent filling the air I'm swiftly moving back to that moment.

He wanted to know the circumstances of how I became stranded and with my clothes drying in the heated cab I find myself pouring out my heart to a near stranger.

"I gambled everything on this man, and I lost," I tell him.

He doesn't interrupt or make any snide comments as I tell him about the matchmaking website I signed up for. Pearl's Mail Order Brides was my hail Mary and talking about how much hope I pinned on it working in my favor is embarrassing.

I mean who decides to become a mail order bride in the modern age? I signed up to marry a man I had never met in person and look how long it took that decision to bite me in the ass. Less than three hours.

And there is no way this mountain man who came to my rescue is going to understand or sympathize. With his body and those soft green eyes there is little chance he doesn't have a girlfriend. I know he doesn't have a wife since he doesn't wear a wedding ring, but I would be foolish to hope that he's single. Or that he would ever consider dating a woman crazy enough to marry a man she knows next to nothing about.

"I didn't sign up," he says once I'm done. "But a lot of my buddies did, and they met their wives through the website. Corey won't stop crowing about it to anyone who will listen."

My head swivels to look at him. His profile is dark, but his voice is soft and soothing like the low rumble of thunder overhead as he tells me about his coworker.

"Willow was running from the Chicago Mafia and Corey has severe social anxiety, so he had a hell of a time trying to date. They met on that website and the rest is history."

"The *Mafia?*" I ask. "Like *The Mafia?*"

"Is there any other kind?" he asks right back.

"I guess not," I reply more to myself than to him.

I can't imagine how terrifying that would be. Certainly puts my little walk in the rain into perspective. Life could be worse. Not that it's good now. I still have nowhere to go and even if I got a flight back to Boston tonight my lease is up, and all my belongings are loaded onto a moving truck.

"Why didn't you sign up?" I ask.

He doesn't need to send for a bride. It's the most obvious answer in the world. He could marry any woman he wanted to. All he would need to do is crook his finger and they would come running. I wouldn't. I do have my pride after all.

The way he talked about his friend's marriage though, there was an almost envious quality in his voice.

"My parents met in a bookstore down in Denver," he tells me. "They both reached for the last copy of the same book and their hands brushed."

Joe has a smile on his face that crinkles the corners of his eyes.

"My whole life they talked about that one moment," he continues. "About how they knew they were meant to be from that one touch. I always thought I would find my wife the same way. The website works for the other guys, but I don't like the idea of finding my bride by looking through a slideshow."

My parents met through an arranged marriage. They never really loved one another. They just talked about loyalty and the importance of family as I grew up. It never felt right. Seeing my friend's parents interact always put a dimmer on my own homelife. My parents didn't grin when they saw each other after a long day. My father spent more time at the bar than he did at home. And my mother was always on the phone chatting with her friends. Neither wanted to be in that house.

As an adult all I wanted was to find a man who would make me want to come home every day with a smile on my face. And I thought that Raymond would be it. Now I'm rethinking the last month. I was willing to settle and that was a mistake. The way my body reacts to Joe's presence is instinctual. It's not something that could be forced with someone else. I should have been searching for a man who could set my body and soul on fire. Not the bare minimum.

The best thing that my ex-fiancé ever did was leave me at the campsite. I would have gone through with our marriage and eventually realized how miserable I was. This just brought me back to reality that much quicker. I could almost thank him.

If he weren't such a giant piece of shit who left me stranded in a storm.

"So where is this guy you signed up to marry?" he asks.

I'm so grateful that he didn't refer to the guy as my fiancé or my husband that I almost miss the stubborn set of his jaw. Looking at him more closely I notice that his shoulders are tensed and he's holding the steering wheel in a white knuckled grip. I know it's not the harsh weather that caused this reaction. The entire time I've been in the truck Jow has been a cautious yet confident driver.

"I don't know," I tell him.

I'm not sure I would tell him if I did know. Joe looks ready to go ten rounds in a boxing match with the man. And I'm going to pretend that it doesn't thrill me.

"He left you up there *alone*?" he asks.

I start to reply but Joe begins to rant. His relaxed manner disappearing like dust on the wind as his earlier grumpiness comes roaring back to life.

"First time in an unfamiliar place. Doesn't know a soul besides him. Packed up your entire life to take a chance on loving him and the bastard just left you stranded at a campsite in that outfit with a storm rolling in with no shelter or way to call for help?"

"Yes," I say.

My voice is low and soft because yes, Raymond is an asshole. But I didn't take any precautions. I shouldn't have left my cell phone in his truck. I should have insisted on going to his house or somewhere public instead of up the bloody mountain.

"When I find him..." Joe's voice trails off before he glances over at me.

Something in my expression causes him to relax his grip on the wheel and I watch as the tension in his body bleeds away.

"Never mind," he says. "You're safe now and that's all that matters."

I watch as we drive down the mountain, the trees lining the road swaying in the wind and the black pavement in front of us shining from the rain. It's several minutes later before Joe clears his throat to catch my attention.

"Did you book a room at the inn or at a hotel down in Bramble?" he asks.

I fight the urge to blush. He's not looking at me but if he were he would see the shame written plain on my face. There's nothing shameful about moving in with a man. But there is shame in the fact that I trusted this man blindly and did not book a room as backup.

Honestly, Raymond could have been a serial killer, and I would be dead right now. This was the *worst* idea I ever had. And to think that I arranged it all and never made a backup plan. I really took a leap without fearing for the fall. Foolish from beginning to end.

"Ah," he says after my silence stretches on too long. "You were getting married today."

"I didn't," I blurt out. "We were supposed to, but he wanted to go camping instead. I didn't know that was his plan. I wore this outfit because we were going to the courthouse first thing. I would *never* wear something like this camping."

Joe is quiet for a moment. I look at him from beneath my lashes to find him stealing glances at me. Those dark green eyes follow the length of my bare legs down to the strappy mud-covered white wedges before they snap back to the road in front of us.

"You make a beautiful bride," he says after a moment. "Prettiest I've ever seen."

It's a terrible lie. Besides the mud, the rain has ruined my hair and makeup, and I know I look a mess. But there is genuine warmth in his tone, and I find myself wishing he had seen me fresh off the plane instead of walking down the road in a downpour. It's a ridiculous fantasy, but all the same I wish it were Joe I had come here to marry.

"The inn isn't going to have a vacancy with all the campers having to evacuate for the storm. And I can't run you all the way down to Bramble because I'm on call tonight."

I start to tell him he can drop me off anywhere in town. Maybe I can borrow his phone and call a taxi or rideshare to take me down to a hotel in Bramble. I never get that far though because he quickly offers a solution.

"You can stay at my cabin," he says. "It's not a luxury hotel or anything but it's got plenty of room."

"I can't." My refusal is immediate. The desire to agree is swift and strong but I'm already weak at the knees for this man. Spending the night in his cabin might be enough to break me.

"It's no trouble," he adds. "And if you don't feel safe, I can spend the night at one of my buddies."

"I'm not afraid of you." It's important that he knows that. "It's just such an imposition. I already made your day harder."

"You did nothing," he replies. "That asshole would have been charged with murder if anything had happened to you. You could have been hit by a car or a bear could have mauled you and you would have been defenseless to either."

"There are really bears out here?" I ask in a squeaky voice.

I walked around for hours at the camp site hunting for birds. Ornithology has always been a peculiar hobby of mine. When Raymond and I didn't click right away I thought it wise to take a step back and walk around for a bit to cool off. I wouldn't have wandered so much if I had known there were bears.

"Yes," Joe answers. "But they tend to avoid people. We're the ones living in their world not the other way around."

I should refuse his offer and insist he drop me off at the little coffee shop I saw on the way to the campsite or at the police station. But I don't.

Joe

C orey is going to laugh his ass off. I gave that man shit for weeks when he told me about how he and Willow met. Dude had to negotiate with a mafia boss to keep his wife from getting murdered. Of all the mail order brides who have come to Crescent Ridge seeking love she has the craziest past.

I told him I would never marry a mail order bride. And sometime in the near future I'm going to become a liar. Figures I would find the woman of my dreams after she came to our town to marry a different man.

She's quiet as I drive us back to my cabin. I already radioed the captain to let him know that all the campsites are clear. While I might be on call, chances are slim that I'll be called out tonight. I'm not going to say that out loud though. No need to jinx myself when I'm taking Miranda back to my home for the first time.

Pulling into the driveway of my cabin, I try not to be too obvious as I check Miranda's reaction. Some of the men who live out this way have modern houses with just a touch of rustic décor. My cabin looks like it was made from a set of Lincoln Logs with a green metal roof. Rustic isn't a strong enough word. Primitive is closer.

The porch light creates a warm circle of yellow light that is just bright enough for me to see how her face lights up as she looks at the cabin. I built it myself five years ago with Corey and Shawn's help. Most of the wood came from my land. The rest came from the Carmichael lumberyard. It might not have a glass wall with a gorgeous view, but it has its own charm.

"You really are a mountain man, aren't you?" she asks.

Her voice is a tad breathy. Like she's terrified that she just went home with a man who might be an axe murderer. Or like she's aroused.

"It's nicer on the inside," I tell her. "Has all the amenities even Wi-Fi, which is no easy thing to get up here."

"It's nice on the outside too," she says.

I turn to look at her only to find her looking at me instead of the cabin. Suddenly her words take on an entirely different meaning. Blood rushes south and I know if she were to look down at this moment it would be impossible for her to miss my reaction.

Miranda doesn't look down. She just fixes me in place with a vulnerable look in her dark eyes. A better man would have taken her to the inn. There is no way they're fully booked. Not once in my life has that happened. And if it were to be full, she could still stay at the resort. No, I'm not a good man. I'm entirely too selfish. A small piece of me believes if I get her into my cabin for a night she might stay for a lifetime.

Those big brown eyes are only adding fuel to the idea. Peering up at me like I'm some kind of hero when everything I want to do to her is pure wickedness. It's the downward flick of her eyelashes as her gaze drops in disappointment that delivers the killing blow to my resolve.

Her lips are soft and supple under mine. Our first kiss is brief. I'm pulling away before her lips move against mine, and in the next second her hands are in my hair and she's gripping the strands tight enough to hurt. When her lips press against mine, I'm willing to forgive her for anything. She kisses just as fiercely as she argues. It's a deliberate and focused siege that steals my breath and my sanity in equal measures.

When we part, I linger a breath away, my eyes still closed as I try to commit every detail to memory. I don't know what she's wearing that smells like mangoes, but I like it.

"Let's get you inside," I say finally.

It's a cop out but if I address the kiss right now, I'll get carried away. I'll be on my knees begging her to exchange one groom for another. And she might want my kiss, might even crave it as desperately as I crave her, but I harbor no illusion that she's willing to take a chance on another man so soon after a betrayal.

She waits patiently, dark eyes tracking my progress, as I circle the truck and open her door. Her hand is small in my grip, her fake nails long and painted in a dark red that matches her lipstick. After helping her down I grab her suitcase despite her protest and then we make a run for the covered porch.

Clothes mostly dry thanks to the truck's heater, the trees block enough of the rain that we don't get completely drenched by the time our shoes hit the pine boards. Miranda waits by the door as I attempt to knock some of the mud off my boots.

"It's unlocked," I tell her.

Her eyes open wide in shock, and I nearly laugh.

"This isn't the city," I tell her. "Most people keep their cars and houses unlocked. If anyone really wanted in my cabin they could bust in a window and climb inside."

"You put a lot of trust in your neighbors."

"I suppose," I say as I follow her inside. "Once Dean Saunders was walking on a trail over by the Jergens house and got chased by a momma bear. They weren't home but their house was unlocked. He swears up and down they saved his life."

Miranda still seems skeptical but I'm not going to press the issue. She can think I'm too trusting.

"You can sleep in here," I call out behind me as I lead her to my bedroom.

Her pink suitcase looks out of place in the room. I have a deer head mounted on the wall that I can see her eyeing.

"The first deer I took when I started hunting with my dad."

Her pause is long as she chooses her words.

"Nice."

I bite my lip to stop myself from laughing. She hates it and that's fine. It was a choice to put taxidermy in the bedroom. One I'm sure most people would find odd.

"Would you like me to move it?" I ask.

"No," she replies. "I'll only be here for a night. It's your room."

"Miranda."

The stern tone pulls her attention away from the taxidermy.

"I can move it," I tell her. "If it makes you uneasy, I would be happy to move it."

"Really?"

"Consider it done."

Her pleased smile is warm, and her bottom lip is still plump from earlier. I want nothing more than to kiss her again, so I clear my throat and show her the ensuite.

"Get comfortable and use whatever you like of mine. While you're in there I'll move the deer and whip up something for dinner."

She dances past me with a grin on her face, stopping only briefly to give me a chaste kiss on my cheek. The shower cuts on a second after she closes the door, and I smile as I get to work.

The head is heavier than I remember but it only takes a few minutes to remove it. I'll need to take some time tomorrow to mount it properly somewhere else, but for now I leave it in the spare bedroom. I've used the space for several hobbies over the years. From trying to find the patience and steady hand to create ships in bottles to a very brief stint with crochet, the room is full of odds and ends.

No bed though. I've never had reason to have a house guest. My parents live in Bramble and any of my friends who have stayed over have used the couch.

I'm taller than the couch is long, but I'll make do. Better I spend the night on the couch than for Miranda to be uncomfortable. She's been through enough today.

Miranda

I wake up before Joe. The hardwood floor is ice cold beneath my feet and I steal a pair of wool socks from his dresser before I venture out of his bedroom. I hear his snoring before I see his bare feet hanging over the arm of the couch. The wool socks muffle my steps as I make my way to the kitchen. The chicken alfredo that Joe made last night was delicious, but I want to make breakfast for him today.

He let me stay with him and take over his bed. Even moved that deer carcass out of the room for me. The least I can do is make him breakfast.

Toast, bacon and eggs sunny side up are plated by the time Joe stumbles into the kitchen. His long brown hair is tangled, and his eyes are barely open.

"Morning," he greets me.

He slides into a seat at the table, knocking his knee against one of the legs as he does.

"Ouch," I sympathize as he winces and rubs his leg.

His face lights up when I slide the plate in front of him. The two eggs positioned above the stack of bacon create the image of a smiley face.

"You didn't have to cook," he tells me.

"I wanted to," I reply.

He digs into the food with a relish I find endearing.

"How do you take your coffee?" I ask as I pour us each a mug.

"Creamer in the fridge," he says between bites. "Pour it until it's the color of caramel candy."

I follow his direction, pouring a *healthy* amount of creamer into his mug. I giggle when I notice the flavor is peppermint mocha. We're in the middle of summer and this man is drinking a flavor more suited to winter and Christmas. I doubt his coffee even tastes like coffee. Probably tastes like a cup of hot cocoa at this point.

My coffee stays black. The coffee grounds I found in his pantry are decent enough not to need any cream or sugar to hide the flavor.

"Perfect," he praises.

I eat my own food and sip my coffee while watching him devour his breakfast. This is my second cup, or I would be in the same state. I need my caffeine to get my day started.

"I need to make some calls, but Raymond has my phone," I tell Joe. "Can I borrow yours?"

Without a word he jumps up from the table abandoning his half-eaten breakfast. He comes back with his cell phone and hands it to me before sitting down again.

"You didn't have to get it right this second."

"No, I didn't but I wanted to," he says.

"Passcode?" I ask.

"No password," he replies. "I only carry it for work. I have to go in today will you be okay here?"

"I can leave-" I start to say.

A quick shake of his head cuts me off.

"You can stay," he says. "Make all the calls you need to, and I'll leave you a number to get a hold of me at the station."

"Couldn't I just call 911?" I joke.

He fixes me with a stern stare and points a finger at me in reproach.

"We don't tie up the emergency line," he says in a playful tone. "Too many idiots on this mountain to risk it."

Joe is gone less than an hour later. He only left after I assured him I was fine at least ten times. I had to promise to call him if I needed anything, and he insisted that I give him Raymond's full name. He promised not to contact the police and only to approach my ex to get my phone back. The dark look in his eye left me feeling skeptical that he would leave it alone at a simple request, but I have people I need to call, and I don't have their numbers memorized.

It's sweet of him to let me stay at his home while I get my life sorted out. My good mood evaporates when I call the moving company. I get put on hold and transferred a dozen times before I finally get someone on the line who can help me.

"Can it be stored at a warehouse?" I ask.

"No ma'am. It has to be delivered to the address on the contract or to another address you verify. We only move your belongings. We do not store them."

It's noon when Joe walks in the door and I'm curled up on the couch trying not to spiral. The woman on the phone was direct and by tomorrow all my stuff will either be in Raymond's house or on his lawn.

"What's up Buttercup?" Joe asks leaning over the back of the couch.

He looks good in the form fitting black T-shirt that looks tight enough on his biceps to cut off circulation.

"The moving company can't store my stuff. My lease is up so I can't have them deliver it all to my old apartment."

"So, all your stuff is going to that bald headed prick's house?" he asks.

"Yes," I groan.

A second later I realize he must have found Raymond. I never told him the man was bald.

"Did you-"

"Yes."

He hands me my phone with a grin. I spot the torn skin on his knuckles, but I don't comment. I'd rather not know.

"Just give them my address," he says. "I'll write it down for you."

"I can't," I immediately protest.

"Your lease is up and what are the chances of you being able to find an apartment for rent in Crescent Ridge in just a few hours?"

He's right. I hate it but I haven't been able to produce a solution in the hour since I got off the phone with the moving company.

"Your ex will move when his contract is up," Joe reasons. "And Crescent Ridge is a beautiful town to live in. Give it a chance."

Despite his gruff exterior I can hear the unspoken plea in his voice.

Give me a chance.

And I want to. Despite everything that has happened in the last twenty-four hours, I want to.

"Okay," I agree. "If, you're sure."

"Utterly," he assures me.

"Thanks for bringing my phone," I tell him. "You didn't have to waste your lunch to get it back to me."

"I didn't," he says. "I was already coming home for lunch if just to see your pretty face."

He laughs when I blush. I follow him to the front door and before he leaves, I stand on my tiptoes and drag him down for a quick kiss goodbye. Or at least what was supposed to be a quick goodbye kiss. My spine presses against the door frame and my legs wrap around Joe's waist before we part minutes later. The hard line of his cock presses against my center with the most delicious pressure despite the denim and cotton layers between us. His cheeks are just as red as mine and his lips are a deep pink from my kisses.

"Gotta go, Miranda," he whispers into the space between us. "My boss will have my ass if I blow off the rest of my shift."

My feet slide down to the floor reluctantly even as I try to catch my breath. Last night wasn't a one off. His kiss really does just set me ablaze with the slightest touch.

"Damn if you don't make me want to risk his wrath," Joe says before pressing one last quick kiss to my lips before darting off the porch and running towards his truck.

The rain, which has come in spurts over the last day, has slowed to a drizzle. His yard is muddy and the smell of petrichor and pine is strong. It's so cozy, here in this warm log cabin watching the rain fall from the windows. I'm sure that in the winter it's even more beautiful.

Four hours later, Joe is back, and my stuff is scheduled to be delivered tomorrow. My friends all know that I am alive and that I am not marrying the asshole who abandoned me on top of a mountain with no shelter and no way of getting to safety. Last I heard Cassie was going to contact the agency and make sure he was permanently banned from the site. The chili I made for dinner is just as much a crowd pleaser as the eggs and bacon from this morning.

"You really don't have to cook," he told me again.

"I like cooking," I reply. "I just never felt like I had time. I was burned out and I refused to admit it, so I dug my heels in at my job and I put in even more hours."

"What else do you like?" he asked later as we sat on the couch watching TV.

"Bird watching," I confess.

"We get quite a few birders coming through chasing a Big Year."

"No, shit?" I ask. "I always wanted to do one, but I barely get to see more than seagulls and pigeons in Boston."

"Travel is key," he replies. "Or so I've heard."

"Well, yes."

"I always wanted to travel. I've never left Colorado," he adds.

"I'd love to see the redwoods in California."

He makes it easy like that. To just talk about the hobbies I enjoy or places I want to see. He doesn't tease me for wanting to spot birds or for wanting to visit a national park rather than go to the beach. Not even Cassie understands my obsession with nature.

"You love nature, but you don't want to go camping?" Joe asks.

"Point to a person who likes sleeping on the ground and I will call you a liar," I reply. "Also, I was in a sundress and wedges! Not an ideal outfit, Joe."

"Noted," he says. "I promise to never take you camping without an inflatable bed and appropriate clothing."

And just like that the lighthearted conversation is gone and the tone has shifted. I've spent more time thinking about kissing him than I'd care to admit. It's insane. We haven't talked about the kissing, and I don't think I want to. My life is just too messy right now.

So instead of talking about our feelings I lean forward and press my lips to his. Right now, I'm right where I want to be. Joe's lips slide hungrily across mine as he slips closer until I'm pressed against his chest.

My hands crawl up his chest taking in every inch of sculpted detail as I peel his shirt up. Warm and smooth to the touch, Joe has hair on his chest in the same dark shade as his beard. He pulls away from our kiss to fling the shirt across the room.

"I can shave it, if you don't like it."

I slide my hand into the patch and grab onto the strands none too gently.

"Don't you fucking dare," I growl. "And don't touch the beard either."

His unrepentant grin is so cocky I nearly bite him.

"So possessive," he whispers. "It's just hair. It'll grow back."

"Or you could just leave it alone, so I'm not stuck looking at a ken doll for the next month."

He laughs, the sound echoing around the living room and filling me with mirth until I'm laughing too. I only stop when he grabs my waist and pulls me down until I'm lying on the couch underneath him.

"Tell me Miranda," he says against my lips all traces of humor replaced by hunger. "Do you taste as good as you smell? I've had your scent imprinted on my brain since yesterday and I'm dying for a taste of your sweet pussy."

"Yes, yes yes," I chant even as Joe peels my leggings down taking my panties with the stretchy cotton.

Not a second later, he's between my thighs. My calves rest on his broad shoulders as he uses to fingers to spread my pussy open so that the first touch of his tongue lands directly on my clit.

The man doesn't dance around the area, playing coy or trying to tease me. No, he licks me in different rhythms with varying pressure until he discovers exactly what I like. And then it's a full-blown assault on my senses. My blood is pumping until I can only hear its roar in my ears, even above my own moans and whimpers.

It doesn't take long for me to stop caring about being too loud or too violent. All I care about as I pull and tug on his hair is getting his tongue to touch me with just the right pressure at just the right angle while I grind against his face.

His comfort is forgotten as I ride a wave of bliss over the edge, and I come with a scream.

"Just as sweet," Joe says before he scoops me up from the couch.

He carries me through the house to the bedroom with ease as I lay boneless in his arms. With only my shirt on I slide into his bed with the plan to return the favor and suck his cock after a nice nap. When he goes to pull away and leave, I catch my finger on the belt loop of his jeans.

"Stay."

"If you're sure," he says.

"Utterly."

Joe

Life with Miranda is nothing short of a dream. The day after we spent the night tangled in the bed the moving truck arrived. I can now proudly say that the spare bedroom can officially be classified as a guest room since it has a bed.

I set it up with its heavy oak headboard and sloping footboard that Miranda insisted made it a sleigh bed. No one has slept in it since it was set up. Every night for the past two weeks I've joined Miranda in what I'm already considering our bed. Sometimes our goodnight kisses turn into more and sometimes we fall asleep before any mischief can begin.

But every morning begins the same way.

"Morning," I purr into her ear.

She grumbles in return, but I know that by the time I step into the shower she'll be right behind me. It might be her modus operandi to start each day in a grumpy manner but by breakfast she's back to her usual sunshine self. I'm dead certain it's the coffee that completes the transformation from a medusa into a normal human woman.

"You've taken such good care of me," Miranda purrs in my ear as she drags a soapy hand up my chest.

It's pure truth. I've done my best to see to all her needs. The mounted deer is a permanent fixture in the guest room, we went to the grocery store and picked up all her favorite snacks and foods, and I've even helped her look for a job here in Crescent Ridge.

"And you've never let me take care of you."

Her hand travels further south until it wraps around my cock in a surprisingly firm grip.

"Miranda," I pant either from the steam of the shower or the intoxicating touch of her, I don't know which. "You don't have to-"

"I want to."

That's quickly become just one of many of *our* things. Little moments that have built a soft spot in my heart. Because for the last two weeks I've made it perfectly clear that she doesn't need to do anything. I didn't pleasure her expecting an equal and swift return. I didn't expect a return at all. She made it clear that she wasn't ready for sex and I'm fine with the way I've been spending my nights.

Long languid moments spent sipping her honeyed arousal between those thick penny-colored thighs.

Leaning back against the tile of the shower I'm breathless as Miranda sinks down to her knees in front of me. The sight of her taking my cock, now fully rinsed of soap, into her mouth is all the more exhilarating because it's her choice.

"Your mouth feels so good," I tell her as she takes me deeper.

Her curls are heavy with water, but not even full submersion can flatten them completely. Wrapping my hand in the umber strands I guide her at a slow pace. Each pull of her mouth sends need ratcheting up my spine.

I'm not going to last long with her delectable mouth wrapped around me. Not when she swirls her tongue around the crown of my cock while peering up at me with false innocence in her mahogany eyes.

"Just like that," I praise when she hollows her cheeks.

Two more minutes of heaven and then I'm tugging her away as my seed splashes across her chest. The milky white creates a pale sheen over her brown skin before it's washed away.

"I wanted to taste it," she grumbles as I help her to her feet.

"Next time," I promise even as I slide my fingers through her slick folds.

No amount of snark or sass can hide the desire in her gaze as I slip first one then two fingers inside her tight sheath. One day I'm going to bury my cock there and stay for hours. Her muscles will grip my cock even tighter than they do my fingers as they piston inside her, seeking that magical spongy spot that will have her come undone in my arms.

The first brush of my fingers against it has her gasping and clawing at my shoulders. Her nails piercing the skin as her back arches and seconds later her channel pulses, milking my fingers exactly as they would my cock as she comes with a husky low moan.

Later when we're thoroughly washed and rinsed, we have breakfast. Miranda's hair is pulled into a messy bun with her scarf keeping her hair out of her face. She has a nail appointment tomorrow, and I'm mentally compiling an argument that's going to convince her to let me buy her a car so that she doesn't have to constantly work around my schedule.

"Once I can find a job, I'll be out from under your feet in a month tops," she says between bites of her oatmeal.

The words catch me off guard. After everything we shared, I didn't think she still planned to leave. I thought we were *together*. Her stuff is mostly unpacked. Half of the closet is filled with her clothes and the same for the large cedar dresser. Her cosmetics and hair care products dominate the bathroom and just last week she bought a bird feeder to hang in the backyard.

I'm spiraling imagining just how easy it's going to be for her to leave me. The bird feeder hangs from a wire, that's simple to remove. Her furniture is heavy and large, but I'll help the loaders move it up. Hell, I'll move it to her new place with my truck. I can't deny her anything. Not even this.

Should have put her name on the mailbox and my ring on her finger. I can wait for sex. But I don't want to go backward, to lose our momentum and have her move out. Maybe she needs some of her independence back. Her own space. She's taken to Crescent Ridge with enthusiasm. Spending her time with the station wives and at *Bean There.*

She no longer has to worry about an awkward run in with her ex. His construction crew finished their project and moved on to the next last week.

I'll never tell her the awful comments that lowlife made when I approached him to get her phone. A man of my word, I had every intention of being civil if curt, but the bastard couldn't keep his mouth shut. False advertising he said. Called Miranda a prude among other things and I lost it.

While she might not want me, she deserves better than him and I'm glad she'll never have to look at his face.

She's looking at me oddly and I realize that I never replied. Normally she's the quiet one in the mornings and I'm chipper because the day is young, and no one has set anything on fire yet.

"Whatever makes you happy," I say finally.

If my tone isn't colored with its usual warmth, it's because it's been scooped out of my heart with an ice pick and a snow shovel. With all heat siphoned out all that's left is cool numbness.

"I'm on mandatory overtime today," I tell her as I leave the table to wash my plate. "I'll be home late so don't feel like you need to wait up."

"I want-"

Leaving her in the kitchen I don't hear the end, but I know it all the same.

I want to.

But I know that's a lie. If she wanted me, she wouldn't be trying so hard to leave. If our time together meant anything to her, she wouldn't be able to just waltz out of my life. I didn't push for sex because I'm not an asshole. I didn't want what we were building between us to feel transactional. Because it wasn't. If Miranda decided she didn't care for me and didn't want my touch or my kisses I would have slept in the other bed. Or moved back to the couch. The shared showers, the talks of future camping trips, all of it now feels cheap.

I feel cheap.

That moment in the shower when I thought she was sucking my cock because she wanted to please me. I thought she was beginning to love me.

For me it happened that first day. Somewhere between spotting her on that roadside and her yelling at me I fell head over heels for the woman. And now my chest is splitting in two exposing my raw heart for the world to see.

The guys at the station give me a wide berth after the first time I snap. I know I'm being cantankerous and surly. I left without saying goodbye for the first time and it hurt more than it helped. I didn't want her to see me break apart at the mention of her moving out.

She hasn't found a job yet. Not many opportunities for an HR manager in Crescent Ridge. I should suggest she look in Bramble but I'm a selfish bastard willing to devour any breadcrumb she'll give me. I want to keep her close. Even if she doesn't love me. Even if she'll eventually fall in love with someone else, I want her in my life.

It's only when I return home from a particularly grueling shift, we lost one of the old farmhouses on Pickney to an electrical fire, that I realize Miranda has caught on to my bad mood. Makes sense. I've done such a half assed job of hiding it. After the last two weeks, with as much soul bearing as I've managed, she knows me better than anyone else.

"Welcome home," she says as she twirls into the living room wearing a lemon print apron. It matches the tea towel set we bought and the oven mitts. I thought she was making a stylistic choice for our home but, she was just helping me pick out things she views as necessities.

"Miranda, we should talk."

My words brought her to an abrupt stop. The joyful smile wiped clean off her face.

"Can it wait until I cut the cake?" she asks.

"You baked a cake?" I ask even as I noticed the smudges of flour and cocoa on her apron.

"Sure did," she replies her grin returning like a slow sunrise on a frosty morning, "From scratch."

I almost tell her she didn't have to bake it, but I bite the words back. How easy it would be to fall back into our routine. She sees it in my expression nonetheless.

"I wanted to," she tells me.

I don't know if it's the scent of chocolate wafting from the open kitchen door or the soft look in her eye that breaks me. All I know is that one minute I'm stone cold with an icy heart, no volcano could melt and the next I'm a wreck.

"You can't bake cakes and cook me breakfast and shower with me and let me lick your pussy all to turn around and leave me."

Miranda

I fidget with the string of my apron. Joe's words hit my chest like a sucker punch. He doesn't get it. I don't *want* to leave. But what if he's just settling for me because it's convenient? Mail order bride delivered to the wrong address.

"I didn't want to be a burden," I tell him, struggling to put my thoughts into words. "You've done so much for me. I can't keep monopolizing your home."

I can't stay where I'm not loved.

A weary hand runs down his face.

"You could never be a burden, Miranda."

"I don't have a job!" I shout. "I can't pay rent and I'm just running up your utilities."

The look he fires my way is impatient at best. Like *I'm* the one who is clueless. He took me in like a stray he found not a woman he dated and asked to move in. I love him. But I need to know that he loves me too.

His green eyes light up nearly incandescent as he looks at me. Spine straightening until he stands tall once more, a far cry from the frumpy slouch he left the house with this morning.

"Do you honestly think that I would let any stranded hiker move in with me?" he asks, catching me off guard.

"You let me," I mumble.

Stepping closer he closes the distance between us as he cups my cheek with a calloused hand.

"You're the exception, Miranda," he says. "I don't want you to move out. Not now. Not *ever*."

The look in his eyes is soft, promising me the moon if he can manage it and there is something about that vulnerability that makes me almost defensive. Because he can't love me. Not after only two weeks. He wasn't even looking for a wife. Let alone some random woman to come crashing into his life and rearranging all the pieces.

Like the deer head he's had since he was a teen that he moved for my comfort.

"Joe," I say abruptly, "You haven't known me a month-"

"I didn't sign up for a bride," Joe interrupts. "But I wanted one. I just wanted serendipity. To find my soul mate in the wild, not doom scrolling through a list of profiles, and it worked. I found you in the middle of nowhere but just like my parents I knew then."

His confession shocks me into silence.

"I want you, Miranda."

"Joe..." my words trail off as my vision blurs with tears.

His thumb brushes aside the streaks as they run down my face but it's no use. I'm a full-blown sprinkler at this point.

"I knew you were the one the second I saw you stomping down that mountain in your wedges dragging that pink luggage of yours."

"Shut up," I say.

"Nope," he grins. "You Miranda Garcia are meant to be mine. If you want to move out and get yourself a rental, I'll help you move, but I guarantee we'll be packing you up and moving you back in before too long."

The way he smiles at me all soft and warm settles me, grounding me to this moment.

"Hardly seems worth the effort," I manage to say.

"It's your call."

I can see in his expression that he's sincere. If I choose to leave, I'll have his full support. And that's enough to tell me exactly what I need to know. For the first time, loving a man doesn't feel like a gamble.

"I love you," I confess.

It's the only response I can give. I'm so helplessly outright in love with this man that I can't stand it.

"I love you too, Miranda," he says against my lips. "My heart is utterly, entirely, unconditionally yours for as long as you'll have me."

Forever.

The word gets lost on my tongue as his lips move over mine. Swift heat courses through my body as he gives me long addictive kisses, one steamrolling into the next.

"You'll stay?" he asks when we break apart to breathe.

"Yes."

"Good, good," he says. "So, cake?"

We've done enough talking. Letting my actions speak for themselves I grab his hands and tug him towards the bedroom. The cake needs to cool down anyway before I cover it in frosting.

Never let it be said that Joe is slow on the uptake. The man's fingers are quick and nimble as he unties my apron leaving it in the hallway. Just as fast, he finds the zipper of my dress once we're in the dark room, only the light of the moon shining through the open drapes above the bed letting me see the dark outline of the man undressing me.

He presses open mouth kisses down my spine for every inch of skin that the zipper reveals until he reaches the small of my back. The dress drifts down to the floor leaving me entirely bare besides the tiny scrap of green lace soaking between my thighs.

I hear rustling behind me and turn to find Joe unbuttoning his orange flannel. The grey T-shirt underneath joins the pile of clothing with a careless toss. Even in the dark room I can see the wicked gleam in his eyes as he prowls towards me. Goosebumps sprout along my arms and a pulse of heat throbs low in my belly, the scent of my arousal apparent over his own pine and leather scent.

There is a dark covetous look in his eye as his gaze scours my body. He's seen me naked every day but there is something in this moment that makes it feel like the first time.

"Off," I order tugging at the waistband of his jeans.

Sitting down on the red plaid sheets I lean back on my elbows to watch him strip.

His belt snaps open with a careful flick of his calloused thumb. The low whine of his zipper is the only sound other than our breath. I've seen his cock. I've stroked and licked it. But I still wait expectantly for him to reveal it. His jeans slide down his muscular legs, the wiry hair on his legs matching his beard and chest hair. Black boxers join the puddle at his feet as he finally exposes the long length of his cock.

The base matches the rest of his golden-brown skin but as it tapers towards the tip it turns a bright cherry red as it curves into a mushroom shaped head. He gives it a rough downward stroke from the tip to the base before following me to the bed.

"I've dreamed of this," he tells me. "Of you spreading those pretty little thighs and letting me take you until the only name you remember is mine."

"Joe," I chide.

Conveniently I ignore the way my dusky brown nipples bead into hard points at his words. He isn't fazed by my criticism if anything it emboldens him.

Settling between my thighs his cock rubs against the lace of my panties before he tugs them aside. One of his fingers slides through my folds gathering the slick evidence of my arousal before using it to lubricate his cock. Seeing the shiny length primed and ready sends another wave of desire burning through me. As my clit tingles in time with my heartbeat it feels like a wire is connecting it to my nipples. A wire pulling more taunt with every passing minute as pleasure builds in my body.

"Are you going to be good, Miranda?" he asks.

While he waits for my answer he drags the swollen head of his cock through my folds, teasing my clit with each pass.

"Maybe," I whisper.

"Hm."

With a shallow thrust of his hips, the tip slides inside me briefly before he pulls back.

"Joe!" I snip.

"Hm?" he hums.

Two weeks of buildup and this man wants to tease me now? When I'm finally underneath him and ready?

"Joe," I growl.

The unrepentant grin that spreads across his face is cocky and full of sinful promise.

"Be good for me," he whispers. "Take every inch and I'll make sure to turn you into a slippery little mess."

"Please," I beg.

The next thrust of his hips delivers on his promise. His cock slides in with ease, all the way to the hilt and I can't help but moan at the rich feeling of fullness as he stretches me.

"That's it," he growls low into my ear. "You take me so well."

"More," I plead.

Giving me exactly what I ask for he withdraws only to come rushing back at once. His cock slides along my walls, building a delicious friction that has me clawing at his back like a wild woman.

He begins to follow that pattern, his hips pumping into mine. As the heat builds, and my spine begins to tingle I wrap my legs around his waist and tilt my hips so that he sinks deeper. The rough glide of his cock hitting just the right spot to drag a moan from the depths of my chest.

Leaning down he kisses me with a gentleness at odds with the brutal grip of his hands on my hips. I fall apart with his name on my lips and soon after he follows me with a roar. Warmth spreads throughout my core as he lets his body rest on mine. Most of his weight is still held up by his elbows but he relaxes enough for his body to settle against mine sharing his warmth.

"Come 'ere," he grumbles in his sleepy voice as he rolls to his side.

He pulls me into the curve of his body until we're spooning, every inch of our bodies pressed together.

"Love you Miranda," he whispers into the shell of my ear.

His warm breath causes the curly strands behind my ear to tickle my neck, and I let out a little giggle.

"Love you, Joe," I whisper back.

He might already be asleep, but I'll tell him again in the morning. And the next day and the next. Because now I know that fate has brought me to the right place at the right time. I might have taken an offbeat route to get here but all that matters is that I made it. And now I have my very own grumpy mountain man to love.

Epilogue

Joe

One Month Later

"Miranda," I say to my fiancée. "Are you sure you don't want me to wear a suit?"

"No, don't be silly," she tells me, "You don't own a suit."

"I could buy one," I mutter.

She drags me closer by the collar of my flannel and promptly slaps my cowboy hat on my unruly hair.

"I'm marrying you, Joe," she says. "I don't want our wedding to look like a Pinterest board or a magazine lay-out. I want you just as you are."

She adjusts my shirt and tilts my hat just so and I stand there on the cobblestone steps of the courthouse as she fusses over me.

My mother and father watch from the shade of a dogwood tree with fond smiles. The day after Miranda and I confessed our love I took her down to Bramble for her nail appointment and brought her by their house for dinner.

It was love at first sight.

Building that relationship with my parents has been good for my bride. She's blossomed into a carefree and restless soul that brightens everyone's day. The guys down at the station like to tease that I'm the rain cloud to her sunshine but I don't mind much.

They don't need to know the details. If they think I'm a jaded grump so be it. I've never been happier in my life and my bride knows that she's the reason for my happiness. Gruff and stern around the town I'll always have a soft spot for Miranda.

"Ready?" she asks me.

I'm already smiling as I take her hand in mine. I've been ready for today since I saw her walking down the road in that pale pink sundress with her muddy wedges and pink suitcase rolling behind her.

Less than an hour later and the magistrate judge pronounces us as husband and wife to the cheers of my parents and several of the other firefighters and their wives.

"Congratulations!" Gloria shouts dragging Shawn behind her.

The blonde man just grins at me as his wife chats with mine, complimenting her dress and the flowers that Mrs.

Clarke arranged for her. White roses with pink and orange snapdragons that look brighter in comparison to her white sundress.

It's strapless and the hem barely hits her knees leaving plenty of glowing brown skin on display. Miranda has swapped out every bottle of lotion in the cabin for her own personal moisturizing regimen and the difference in my hands alone is astonishing.

Corey slaps my back as he and Willow join the throng of people crowding around us. Until today they were the most recent newlyweds in Crescent Ridge and just like the other couples, they can't keep their hands off each other. Considering that I still have my arm wrapped around Miranda I can't talk. If I weren't needed at the station, she would have to pry me off her with a crowbar and a spatula every morning.

It's as we're walking down the sidewalk on our way to the new steak house that just opened for our reception that my wife gets a devious look in her eye. Our friends and family are several steps ahead, but I still lean down so that she can whisper into my ear.

"Think they'll miss us?" she asks.

Hanging back for a moment I watch as the group turns the corner, and we lose sight of them.

"The reception is more for the wedding guests," I say. "And we already paid for the food and open bar, so I doubt they'll complain too much."

Her giggle is music to my ears as I bend down to scoop her into my arms. I carry her back to the truck as tourists stare and locals laugh. I see Mama Mary wave in our direction, and I know that she'll tell my parents about this before we make it halfway home.

"They'll never let us live this down."

"Maybe not," I reply sliding behind the wheel. "But I'm sure there will be another couple paired off soon and we'll be old news in a month."

"Rumor is Elaine Carmichael is holding interviews for a position at her bakery as a ruse to find wives for her sons," Miranda tells me as we start the short drive home.

My hand lands on her bare thigh as she catches me up on all the local gossip and it's impossible to notice that her voice gets higher the closer my hand slides to her core. By the time I pull into the driveway, Miranda is done waiting. My fingers slip out of her just for her to slide between me and the steering wheel, her thighs landing on either side of mine as she works my cock free of my jeans and boxers.

"Don't move," she orders. "Just sit there and let me ride your cock."

Her words freeze me in place as she lifts her sundress and sinks down on my cock in one smooth movement. She rises and falls, her back arching over the steering wheel while she grabs the sleeves of my flannel for support.

I do my best to follow her wishes, but as she rides me I find myself thrusting up, seeking more of her warmth.

Even as she drenches my cock with her arousal I push for more. Every descent is met with a short powerful thrust of my hips upwards until I'm building a rhythm of her moans. One barreling straight into the next.

She comes on my cock with a scream that startles a nearby nest of mountain blue jays despite the windows being rolled up. I follow immediately after, pumping my seed as deep into her needy pussy as I can.

"Couldn't wait?" I ask later.

"Nope," she replies.

Pressing a soft kiss to her dewy forehead I marvel at the woman in my arms. And how fate was always on my side. I just didn't know it. I might not have gone about it the same way as my buddies, but I certainly found my own mail order bride.

The End

Check out Mountain Man's Reluctant Mail Order Bride to meet Marcus, a working-class snowplow driver and Caroline a disgraced socialite looking for a new start.

***

You can sign up for my newsletter or follow me on Amazon or Facebook to stay up to date on new releases and other updates.

Crescent Ridge Mail Order Brides

Crescent Ridge: Mountain Men In Uniform

A Bride For Thomas

A Bride For Scott

A Bride For Dennis

Crescent Ridge Mail Order Grooms

Pearl's Modern Mail Order Brides

The Lighthouse Keeper's Mail Order Bride

Pearl's Mail Order Brides

Holiday Sweet Treats

Cinnamon Kissed

Sweetheart

Pumpkin Spiced Love

Printed in Dunstable, United Kingdom

72282275R00152